Duff

To Joan,

I hope you enjoy.

All the best,

Suzy

Duff

Suzy Norman

Patrician Press
Manningtree

Suzy Norman was a freelance journalist for the *Daily Mail*, *The Reading Evening Post*, and the *Hackney Gazette*, amongst other newspapers. As a shortlisted author, her fiction appeared in *The Dundee International Book Prize 2014 Cargo Anthology*.

Suzy paints too, mainly body parts, and her photography has appeared in *The Guardian* and at the Royal Academy. She grew up in Monmouthshire then moved to London for her education. She completed her MA at University College London. She lives with her husband and two naughty black cats.

Published by Patrician Press 2015
For more information: www.patricianpress.com

First published as a paperback edition by Patrician Press 2015

E-book edition published by Patrician Press 2015

British Library Cataloguing in Publication Data. A catalogue record for this book is available from the British Library.

ISBN paperback edition 978-0-9932388-4-0

ISBN e-book edition 978-0-9932388-3-3

Printed and bound in Peterborough by Printondemand-worldwide

www.patricianpress.com

For P.J.N.

The force that through the green fuse drives the flower
Drives my green age; that blast the roots of trees
Is my destroyer.

Dylan Thomas

There is a rollicking kindness that looks like madness.

Friedrich Nietzsche

Duff

The bailiff turned around and headed back. Breathless, pink-cheeked and two breaths short of a cardiac, he crunched up the gravel towards the gate. Beyond him, the sky turned from grey to blue. A blackbird cawed its warning.

I was reprieved again, at least for the time being. So, crawling back under my duvet, I stared at the scorched blim-holes in the cotton. With a shaking hand, I dabbed my eyes and gazed out through the brown net curtains. The Black Mountains looked cold and striped through. Cwm, my daughter's pony, blinked in the hard sun. She stared at me – no! Damn well straight through me. She appeared to be swaying. I tell you, much more of this and I'd have to call the Doctor.

I heard the door slam below and the soft pad of footsteps. Angharad came creeping up the stairs and into my room. She held two mugs in her hand. Mugs were all I had, don't ask me why.

'You look concerned,' I said, disgusted at how meek I sounded. 'But you shouldn't worry. It's not as bad as all that.'

Angharad tilted her head and examined me, like I was one of her lab rats. She rubbed her fingers through her hair, sleeked-back and flat to her scalp. She wore new glasses, small, horn-rimmed, mail-order affairs. I watched them slip halfway down her nose. Lazily, I rested my hand on her knee.

'I wasn't going to say anything,' she said.

'The wine – you want us to celebrate?'

'Don't be daft. I just thought you'd welcome the chance to numb the pain.'

She tensed at my touch, so I dropped my hand. The heat was fierce and I peeled down an extra layer of bed sheet. Together, we frowned at the battered shape of my scar, blood-red and bloated, slicing through a pillow of flab. Angharad looked me up and down with pity. She took off her specs. I fought down a tear.

'Tell me about your walks with Honks,' I said. More than anything, I wanted to hear about life on the outside, where the wind blew up the sea.

'Around the Gower, mainly,' she said. 'We just hang out, you know. Caswell Bay on a crisp day with blue skies. You would go too if you could.'

Her voice calmed me. Enjoying myself, I closed my eyes. This was exactly the kind of scene I was happy to picture.

'Honks loves it. He's handy too. Sniffs around the place, wagging his tail.'

She smoothed down her pencil skirt.

'And you know something?'

I didn't, but I was sure she was about to tell me.

'I like collecting rocks, fossils, that type of thing? Well, I found a real beaut, a spiral. I handed it in to the Geology Department.' I watched her smile widen and then wane. I was glad because I'd learned not to trust her smile. She leaned in closer. Her breath was warm and fruity. 'And look, listen, Duff, about the other day.'

Wiping my forehead with a tissue, stiff from over-use, I tried to remember what was said between us the last time she was here. My short-term memory was shot, the fault of the morphine, maybe.

'I couldn't stop them, could I? They were really going on. Said you're lazy. Don't go the extra mile. All sorts of stuff. Said you lied in your interview.'

I scanned her feet, neatly crossed on my threadbare, coffee-stained carpet. Her shoes were a deep, morello cherry. She was on her way to somewhere important. I wondered where. *And who was saying this, exactly?*

'They said you – there was talk of little white lies. Said you mis-sold your skills – made out you knew more than you did.'

She leaned in closer and looked at me a beat too long. Her small eyes were bug-like and suspicious. I sensed a soft air-kiss dying near my cheek.

'Because you know what this is really about, don't you, Duff?'

'?'

'Nerys,' she said with a force that made me swallow. 'She

left you both high and dry. Without a second thought. I've always said she has a cold heart.'

I shivered to hear Nerys's name in this room that used to belong to us, when Nerys had been a part of these four walls too. So, I willed myself to change the subject but I couldn't think of anything to say. Instead, my hand floated towards her. My stiff fingers grabbed her mug and I took a sip. *A cold heart? Well, in that case, darlin', that makes you as cold and hard-nosed as your predecessor. I bet you've only come here for your money.*

Christ, even that limp biscuit Daryl was more help than Angharad about the place. Daryl, at least, had been known to lend me a fiver in return for five minutes alone with my daughter.

Silently, I watched Angharad leave. To who, and to where, I had no idea. I didn't much care.

After she'd gone, I took a puff on my inhaler and breathed out my relief. From the warm comfort of my bed, I looked past my weak, chipped toenails to the starving sheep in the grass – poor, hungry sheep. Slowly, I got up and oared my sorry frame over to the dresser. I shouted down to my daughter, Cara, to make me a sandwich. I waited but there was no answer. Damn. Then I would go out instead, and I tied my rat-gnawed Converse in a double-knot. I grabbed my stick.

In the newsagents, Bob looked up from his greasy, black fringe. When he saw me he pushed his magazine, all pink lettering and bulging breasts, under a glossy. He attempted a smile but Bob couldn't smile properly. He wiggled his lips, but he gave up too easily.

'You better now, Duff? Gave us quite a scare, like.'

I'd been interned in hospital with a fierce bout of pneumonia, a real zinger, held at the mercy of the White Coats. They don't mess around, these people: they flip you over, truss you up, bolt you down with invisible straps. For a week, it had been me versus the ward staff, me versus the carpet, the curtains.

'You have thoughts in a place like that,' I said to Bob, who was at least prepared to offer me his full attention. 'You have ideas.'

'?'

'My wife is back,' I said. 'Or soon will be. Cara said so.'

Bob bounced his palm off his pale forehead, struggling to remember the woman who left ten years ago.

'Your missus with the bum like a cow's arse? Sorry,' he said, but I'd grown used to Bob's outbursts. We all had.

'See, she thinks I'm dying.'

Bob tapped his fingers on his glossy and thought for a moment.

'Wow,' he said, as if he thought this was the reaction I wanted.

But it was no use filling Bob's simple, grey matter with details about my soap opera life. He wouldn't be able to retain them. Lazily, I picked the cheapest chocolate bar I could see before me. There was scant choice – maybe two or three varieties, sprawled across the wooden counter. I handed him my last note and looked around me. If Bob had other customers apart from Cara and me, I would have been surprised, and we only stopped by through loyalty. Everyone else in Betwys went to the new hypermarket on the edge of town. Bob blinked as slowly as a bull.

'Will you bring her in?' he asked. 'When she comes?'

'Fine,' I said, with no intention of doing so. I left him with his nose pressed to the smut. I headed up the hill.

Sinclair hoisted his thumbs in the direction of the only leather chair and I sat down. He shook his shoulders, rolled them forwards, then back, preparing himself. As he bustled out the back, I took a moment to admire the overheads: a pair of rusty-blunt shears; an old dial phone on a scorched table; a sun-bleached Doors poster; a plastic kettle with a broken lid; a chipped dustpan and brush. The place was his whole world, yet it was no bigger than my box room. His molting tabby patted Jones the Warren's grey hair around the broken tiles.

'Flick me one of those will you? My throat's dry *as*.'

I handed him an imperial mint from the dish on the shelf. The mints were dusty. Come to think of it, I don't remember Sinclair ever having offered me a cup of tea.

He hummed, running his fingers through my hair, ramming his thumbs into my temples, keeping them there until I settled back. I watched the dust dance in the light from the window. The particles appeared to slice right through me. At least news hadn't reached this dark corner of the village about my health scare.

'You expect this on tick again, Duff?' he asked knowing full well the answer. Sinclair wasn't his real name. Nobody knew his real name.

'Could I?'

He sighed and I heard his brain ticking: *This really will be the last time, mind.*

'You and Angharad going somewhere special?'

Ah, Angharad.

Already the name sounded like a distant, recurring dream, like the one I used to have about the friendly bear who turned out to be not so friendly. The bear used to growl at me, demanding I return the money – or else.

Sinclair's phone rang. He mopped his brow and clipped close to my ears.

'I have a special visitor. Can't say anything, sorry.'

He glanced at my stick with the chipped handle, thought for a moment and then he twisted his hips left and right.

'What's up?' I asked.

'At my age you have to keep all parts moving. Do twenty hip rotations before bed, too. Don't use it, you lose it.'

I nodded in agreement to Sinclair's reflection in the mirror. So, Sinclair was another one trying to keep hold of his youth. It was true: there was little to do around here other than pump iron. You saw the triangle men, as I liked to call them, making their way along the street, high-fiving anyone who would give one back. The thick blade nicked the lobe of my ear. I yelped. To avoid a repeat, I kept my head up. In the mirror, I saw Sinclair's sunken cheeks warmed through with a tan. My own face was thirsty for colour. My freckles were a faded, cold auburn.

'Goin' away this year, Duff?'

This again. I wanted to laugh – or cry. Some chance.

'Me, I'm off to Croatia. Cheap fun. More for your roubles.'

A skater-boy in a yellow and neon blue vest rolled past the window. Flashing his eyes at us, he slammed his palms on the barber's pole. His pasty knees wobbled for a bit, and then he sped off. Sinclair dropped his cutters with a clang and shouted after him.

When he was done, and my shaved head resembled that of a troubled convict, I slipped my hand in my pocket and offered him all I had. He took my shrapnel and slotted it inside his tip jar. The words HELP ME PLEASE KINDLY TA were scrawled in black ink.

I stepped outside. The dusty wind blew past my ears. Experimentally, I pulled out my battered wallet and gave it a hopeful shake. I realised I had surrendered my last pound to Sinclair. So, with little to occupy me, other than nail-biting anticipation, I headed home to wait for my wife. She would be home in under an hour.

At the farm, I watched the long grass bend in the breeze. I thought of my neighbour, Jones the Warren, and his shed-full of equipment to suit any job, but I knew not to ask to borrow his strimmer again.

Jones the Warren's garden could not have been more different to mine. His was an orderly, manicured paradise. He had long rows of clematis that sprouted in long, black boxes. There were small patches of blue speedwell that ran along hedged borders. The bees hummed.

I breathed in and smelt the air. Absent-mindedly, I kicked the watering can at my feet. I kicked it into the bush and watched the water trickle in a line towards the gate. The gate still bore the mark of our last fight. It was like the farm had recorded the whole story of Nerys and me, not just the happy times.

Above my head, the sky blackened. Splashes from the roof of the campervan wetted my T-shirt. I tightened my fists. The rain had sharp edges.

Inside, I walked through the hall, cursing myself for not bothering to clear away the cobwebs. The washing up was stacked high next to the sink. The place smelt bad. But there was worse still. The bin yawned at me from across the kitchen. My washing was scrunched up in a ball next to the machine. Looking at it, I churned with less purpose than a washing cycle.

I went to the fridge and pulled out the vegetable tray. Brown slush slopped around the plastic and dripped on the slates at my feet. I went to fetch the kettle and looked at the Aga's singed rings. A spider skipped across the top, and dived in the sink, defying me to turn on the tap. I flicked it with my finger and watched it bounce up on to the draining board. I sneered back at it.

On the round table in the centre of the room was my notepad and pen. I thought back to that day, a decade ago, when I'd wanted to kick Nerys right there in the shin, but instead I'd rammed my foot in the gate. I sat down in the same chair she had sat in that day, the fake Rennie Mackintosh… *Ah, cry if you want to, Nerys, it won't make any difference; it won't bring us back together again.*

Upstairs, in my room, I settled in bed, imagining myself on a boat, comfortably adrift. I filled my lungs deep, breathing in the quiet before the storm. There was to be nothing else for it. I rummaged in my bedside table and grabbed a fistful of memories.

I held a bleached Polaroid near to my face and studied this person smiling back at me. The kitchen she stood in was one I remembered well. The table in Nerys's student halls had been buried under oily rags. The chairs had been transformed from plain, rented wood to paint-spattered wonders. My wife had been a brilliant painter once. There'd been a darkness to her work that had impressed me.

Nerys wore blue dungarees. A button missing. Around her nose were tiny, brown circles. I counted them: ten around the bridge, eleven, twelve. Her neck was short, like a pug's. I touched my own and gave it a light squeeze. I stopped. The next picture brought a tear to my eye.

Durham.

Through the window of the train there'd been a rolling tape of grass. Inside the carriage there had been the damp smell of rolling tobacco. Nerys pressed her nose up to the window. A murky bowl, she'd said. But I knew from that point on, as we rolled down south, the view would change. There would be tarmac roads, crowded buildings and concrete.

It had been a rainy-wet Tuesday. She'd taken a swig of my ale and slid her hands down my trousers. Opposite us, an old woman knitted brown squares. Pearl one, drop one, pearl one, drop one. Nerys had kept stroking. Silently, I'd answered her. *Easy now girl, easy does it, easy.*

So, my wife came back, as she said she would. The campervan door flapped open, shut, open-shut. I smiled to see her down on her knees, the Nerys I remembered.

I leaned back, eyeing the middle distance and Jones the Warren mid-way up the hill. He would have his manky, balding sheepdog Fiff with him, although I couldn't be sure. From this distance, he was a resting fly.

My wife dunked her sponge in a bucket, then squeezed. Morning flies skated up and zigged. I levered myself up. She shooed me back and I crashed down into the canvas of my deckchair. She slid her hand across her silver buckles.

'What a state. Good God, Duff, it smells like a rooster died in here.'

'Probably. Although, I think Daryl might have noticed – even if I – '

'Maybe we should have had that road trip,' she said. 'A better use for it than a prison for these stinking roosters.'

Nerys scrubbed round and down. Like a watch hurriedly wound, she pressed and wiped. I admired the veins pulsing in her hands. Cwm nodded his approval, satisfied to have her near. As for me, I jotted down some extraneous thoughts. *The love between us defies time. Ten years? Nothing. Nothing when my draw is a long arm stretched across the heavens. Because the cement hasn't eroded; it might have in the battering rain, but it –*

My wife dunked her sponge and squeezed. I rubbed my eyes. Through the oak tree, the sun beamed a smile – a sign?

The campervan, festooned as it was with flowers and symbols, was my museum piece. A year-or-so ago, I'd considered donating it to the Red Cross or the Buddhist Centre, but no, I'd paid a grand for it in '95, it was my museum piece and it was going to stay.

I launched myself up. Dizzy, I slumped down again. My heart raced at the thought of us together on the road, with no particular place in mind. It was like the van had been here all the while, waiting for a chance like this.

'Hanging out. Kicking off our shoes. Knocking on doors – whatever takes our fancy,' I said. 'So what do you say?'

With her credit card, Nerys scraped droppings from the van floor.

'Just us?' she asked.

'Ay, the nooks and crannies of the country. The stardust, the oddities.'

She dusted off her hands, but her look said: *Honey, you've got to be kidding me, right?*

'And now the waiting is over,' I said. 'Gone, kapish.'

I watched her thrust her hips forward. *Oh sure, honey, waiting for what?* She was trying to attach herself to me. In response, I opened my legs an inch wider, my welcome home present.

'It's been waiting for a day like today,' I said.

'Or a special visitor like me, mug enough to clean it out? Honey, you can be such a fool.'

With Nerys gone, my life had withered. Like rewinding a video tape, the farm had slid into reverse. The plants had shrunk back into the soil. The sheep had receded, melting back into their bones. My efforts to grow the kind of greenery which would have been of any use in the kitchen, or elsewhere, had been an abject failure.

Nerys flicked a ball of fluff. I watched it float up to be swallowed by the birch. She had left me without a word, not so much as a note, *nothing*. Yet this farm belonged to her. I was only here until she sold it.

In celebration of my wife's return, I wanted to howl and do a little dance. Ten years on from the day she left, we would be together again. No distractions, no Cara, no Daryl, the two of us. I watched her face darken, fearful of our past and its pull.

'I can do a Kerouac,' I said. 'Keep a stream-of-consciousness journal. Somewhere between a dream and waking – no?'

My wife threw down her sponge.

'Forget it,' she said with a sharpness that spanked my ears. 'There's no way you're getting me into this thing.'

What I had come to accept was Nerys had the practical skills, the know-how. She understood how to balance the books, the credits, the debits, the ups, the downs. There was our shop too: the customers flocked to her in a way they never had to me. Her good looks didn't harm: men fancied her, women copied her hairstyles – pinned up one week, cropped short the next. The animals pined for her. Hard to describe, even to myself, but Cwm took to winking at me across the fields. I'd watch Cwm from the window of my damp, slate-fronted house. Even the crocuses leaned towards me, breathing her name.

Slowly, my wife smiled. I photographed this smile with my eyes and filed it in the back of my head.

'But you're not – how the hell *can* we? Cara – '

She turned her back on me, looking equally as magnificent from behind as she did from the front. *We can do, this, Nerys. You said so yourself. We were idiots not to. But we couldn't see it.*

'The open road,' I told her. 'The highway with no-one on it.'

'Jeez. You must be kidding, right?'

I remembered Nerys's letter to Cara. Cara at least kept me up to speed with the latest goings-on in my wife's strange life in Santa Fe. There'd been others, I knew that much. There'd been a tycoon, Rupert, who just so happened to be a Scientologist. Cara told me he hadn't hung around long. There'd been an account of a red sports car waiting outside my wife's apartment, ready to speed off when she came to the window. But Cara's account of a man named Taryn gave me cause for concern too. He'd made rich in Bangladesh dabbling in the rag trade. He had been a money-grabbing, sleazy dirt-bag, ruthless and cruel. Cara told me he had two homes: one in Maine, a ranch-style place, and an apartment in Santa Fe. He was thirty-two and handsome with a neat, black beard. I dropped my smile.

'What time will she be back from Daryl's?' I asked.

Nerys turned around. Specks of dust settled on her mustard dungarees.

'She said after six – why?'

With swollen eyes, I shot inside, coughing like a man nearly drowned. In the kitchen, I pulled out a pad and pen. I drew arrows and lines, tiny squares for pitstops. Feverishly, I looked out to the coop Nerys had knocked together. The cockerels stared at me from behind thin wire, disorientated in their new home. Their soulful eyes looked cheated and I felt their pain. A pang of inexplicable melancholy washed over me. *Damn, don't you little chooks… no, don't you look at me that way.*

I sprung back from twitching the curtains and watched my wife loom towards me. Her dungarees swished in the breeze, worn and dusty. I knew she was wobbling under the weight of my idea. Given time she would fall. The power I used to have; I still had it. She strolled in, a chamois leather dangling from her pocket.

'I thought for our first stop – you've never been there. Definitely, you'll like that.'

She slumped down in my fake Rennie Mackintosh chair. Like a metronome, she clicked-clacked love and hate.

'What are you – ? I haven't agreed to a goddamn thing. You're crazy. And what about Cara?'

I twirled my pen and looked at her – one beautiful woman. Slowly, she shook her head, treating me to an easy grin. This threw me. Surely, it couldn't be this easy.

'What about Cara? You're supposed to be – '

'We'll leave a note,' I said.

'But where would we – '

'York. Then straight up.' I showed her the workings in my pad. 'Look here, Durham. You've always wanted to. Then how about Berwick upon Tweed, just for the kicks?'

The air dissolved between us. Her neutral look hardened.

'Duff, you can't drive in your – '

'I'll be the passenger,' I said, determined to keep momentum going. 'You can drive. We'll head up the long stretch of coast to Scotland.'

'I guess you mean Aberdeen?'

Of course Aberdeen. And at this, I was Hercules again. Scotland was the story of our love, where it all began. I knew her weak spots as well as her freckles. She watched me scribble a note, barely legible to my morphined eyes. *Babe, I've left 50 20 pounds in the egg dish to tide you over. Because: guess what? The magic bus is hitting the road! So you be good – and if you can't be good…*

'You're nuts,' she said, blowing her fringe upwards. I watched a money spider dangle above her head, it was unsure whether to stay or drop. Nerys crossed her arms.

I damn well shot upstairs.

In my daughter's room, where due to the mounds of junk in my own room, I kept my clothes, I looked up at the hole in the ceiling. Drops of rain bounced off my head. Scrambling around for my trousers, I looked hard at the peeling walls. I wouldn't be seeing them for a while. With a quick hand, I shoved worn pants and greying t-shirts in a case. I pushed my daughter's things out of my way – her lumberjack shirts, her under-nourished essay on Ulysses – lazy, lazy. I stared at the wall. With a nonchalant puff of his lips, Bob Marley faced away from me and out towards the sheep – to think my bright, beautiful daughter had bought such a cliché – and I listened. There was nothing, only the distant buzz of a strimmer. I closed my eyes and heard my wife drag her case across the kitchen. I heard her unzip it with a sigh. There were to be no more circling thoughts, no more creeping anger. I was sick to the gut with anger.

The last item to be loaded onto the van was my duvet. I patted it flat. From under the passenger seat I pulled out a map, still intact. Nerys snatched it from me.

'Let me see. 1987. Oh boy.'

'Don't tell me, it only seems like yesterday?'

'But this will be as good as useless,' she said. 'The roads will have changed.'

I turned my head around, scanning the bleach-stained van, like I couldn't believe this was all there would be. I watched Nerys let the sun float through her, lighting up her frown.

'A few days and no more. For old time's sake,' she said.

Nerys opened her door and stepped down. So, my plan had been met with little resistance. I couldn't quite believe my luck.

'And don't worry about sleeping arrangements,' I said. 'One word: B&Bs.'

'But the state of you,' she said. 'Honey, your lungs are shot. You'll need to rest on the road. At least some of the time.'

'And you'll be driving,' I said. 'Trust me, it's going to be amazing.'

She slammed the door and I listened to the sloshing of petrol. She took her time about it. When she returned, I detected a determined glint. I watched her start the engine. With a limp fist, I thumped the dashboard.

'Come on now. Don't let us down. Try again, quicker, Cara will be back soon.'

The engine phut-phutted. I had to admit it didn't sound promising.

'I told you,' she said.

'Patience now. One more crank should do it.'

And I watched a wisp of hair escape from under her headscarf.

'I don't believe it – crazy – but we're away. Goddamn it, Duff.'

'See? It just needed a bit of encouragement.'

She shook her head and looked at me in the same way she's always done, a muffled kind of love. We edged up the drive.

'If we make it far enough, will we go on the motorways, or up through the mountains?'

I wondered had she forgotten. Twenty years ago she said, without doubt, we were to go up through the middle. The road past Snowdonia, REM's *Up* on the tape player.

'Stop the van,' I said.

'Huh?'

'The tapes! We can't go without the tapes.'

She tutted, waving the cracked screen of her iPhone at me. This bright, red-letter day of ours: it dazzled. Nineteen years ago, when Cara had fought her way out of Nerys with her lungs sharp and fresh, paled in comparison. I glanced down at her feet, babyish and bare. The spirit in my wife was the same as it always was.

'We'll be the envy of everyone,' I said.

Ahead, the track to the road was gravel-rough. Trees lined the path. They blew in a frenzy to match my fluttering heart. We were kissing goodbye to the green, sloped fields, the bare cupboards and the damp. I couldn't have been happier. I wanted to burn up the path, flags blazing, but instead we tilted left then right, wheezing past stone cottages and sleeping shops. The outside air crept inside the van. I breathed in the leather. Passing shoe leather shone, like wet pebbles.

We hit the A-roads and trundled in the left lane. A Megabus flashed by in stripes of blue and yellow. From the back seat, faces swung round, childish and stupid. My wife would have plenty to tell her students in Santa Fe.

'Goddamn it, Duff. The wheel, it's stiff.'

'Now, judging by this map, we should be in York in just over three hours,' I said. 'Amazing, isn't it? The variety.'

'You're crazy,' she said. 'In this thing? The old beast won't go over forty. I'm surprised the transport police haven't pulled us over for being a danger.'

A mile-or-so before Snowdonia, we spotted a roadside café. Steam hovered above the pavement. A Welsh sign swung in a shard of bronze light. There were backpacks and over-sized boots, the type that chafed my sensitive heels. Olive-skinned school kids formed a line past the van. We watched them file into the café talking a language I didn't understand.

Nerys pulled over and I wondered what there was for her to do in Santa Fe. I suspected it couldn't be much fun hanging with that fashion crowd. We headed inside. Nerys looked around her.

'What have they got here?' she asked. 'Not much. I'll have to have an omelette or a fried egg.'

I grunted at the blow of a backpack to my shoulder. So, my wife was a vegetarian these days. What else didn't I know about her? Angharad was one too. Oh, Angharad, your days as my girlfriend are numbered. Mark my words. I watched my wife order in Welsh, mellifluous and commanding.

'Coffi, cariad,' she said.

'And what if I didn't want coffee?'

We chose a seat near the door.

'Look, it's lovely, isn't it?' Nerys said. 'All windows and long benches. It's basic, so British.'

My anger towards my wife was palpable but I tried to keep it down. My wrists shook and my chest trembled. She would have to win me over, as good as knock me sideways, for me to forgive and forget. She was on trial here, as much as I wanted her.

'So, you're still hell-bent on this in your state?' Nerys asked. 'We're only three hours from home. Still time to head back for a lie down.'

But I knew from her tone, she was only teasing me. She wanted to do this as much as I did. My wife didn't enter into deals lightly. This is what hurt the most. She left me, but I knew she would have thought long and hard about it.

When our coffees arrived, I was certain there was to be no turning back.

So, I'm waiting in the van for Nerys. Her life must be crummy over there in Santa Fe for her to come back so readily. Yesterday, when she'd arrived back, she'd been as pale as tropical sand. In the cold light of my room, she'd peered into my sunken eyes. America had sluiced her hair through with grey and had marked her face with tiny lines. America had given her a voice, but it had taken away her youth.

Nerys was lucky to have me alive and in one piece, I hoped she appreciated the fact. What I really *should* do is exercise my rights as her husband: confront her head-on and say *you really went and hurt me, honey; you really went and dug the knife in deep.* The pain of being abandoned by the woman you needed more than life itself, Christ, I'd never experienced a blow like it. Not the kind of feeling you'd want to have every day. She'd caught me off-guard. A skilful shot into an unmanned goal, Sinclair had said.

I had that choky dryness in my mouth again. Nerys could do that to me, she could make me reach for the water. She had the power. Baby did a bad, bad thing.

I can take a lot, and I *did* take a lot from her. Some women blame you for everything, and what you do is you listen and you swallow it down, no arguments. Yeah, I took *exactly* those kinds of bullets. I willed my anger to simmer down. Maybe it would, maybe it wouldn't, only time would tell.

I watched them file past the bow in their anoraks, the Straights. I missed my smokes a lot. I wanted to suck one down deep, blow smoke through the window, greet them with a casual, dead-eyed stare. That kind of a mood.

She walked slowly towards me, my wife, all high cheekbones, sharp fringe and chunky thighs. At my age, this is exactly the kind of thing you do: you *notice* things; you value them and you're grateful. People are here one minute, gone the next. People can be selfish, manipulative, glorious and deplorable. Nerys was all of these things.

As for her, her eyes saw: I don't know, but I had my own impression of myself. I was all greying sideburns, no longer red; stubby nails where I chewed them down; the average size nine shoes. No great beauty, but no fool either.

I'd been to America once, Los Angeles. Santa Fe, I imagined, would be a lot like that: fake blondes with orange tans, cat-sized portions, everyone a health freak, nothing but a plastic playground and a fool's paradise. Patiently, I watched my wife climb back in the van.

'They made me up an egg roll. That was good of them.'

'Have you been a vegetarian long?'

I watched her roll up her sleeves. She did this before driving, I'd noticed.

'Nope, I wouldn't say so.'

'Tell me, then, how do you socialise? In vegetarian restaurants with other vegetarians? Because that's no kind of a life.'

My wife ignored this but, since being ejected from hospital, I'd had plenty of thoughts like these. They swirled in my head but I couldn't use them. I knew what I needed was to get out more, dip my feet in the water. The world had passed on by for too long. I coughed, a toughie, a real hacker.

'Here, have this,' she said. 'I don't want a casualty on our hands. Not here in the back of beyond.'

I took it from her and slugged. The ice-cold water was soothing down my throat. Lazily, I watched her grope around in her bag and fasten a sponge map to the mirror.

'America, is it… a bit tawdry?'

'Lavender, actually,' she said. 'I know how quickly this place can reek. Neither of us smells too fresh.'

I observed my wife, her curls fluffed with mousse and I knew she'd be thinking ahead, wondering about the next place. With Nerys, this was always the way.

'Goddamn, it's slow,' she said. 'So, Cara, what do you think? Will she be back yet? We shouldn't be doing this. We should have left this until the morning, you know how she can be. Everything has to be just so.'

But I didn't want to think about Cara. Now, here, like this.

'Look,' I said, trying to change the subject. 'Will you stop and look around you?'

Our van became lost in the greyness, as beautiful as it was terrifying. The mountains made a mockery of us, their peaks like judging heads. The further up we went, the heavier the mountains became. Drizzle obscured the tallest. Walkers pulled their hoods tight around their faces, and they whooshed past us until we left them behind. Restlessly, I shifted in my seat. I checked my watch for the third time in as many minutes.

'Here. Grab this for me, will you?' she said.

Nerys handed me her phone. In my fever, I'd forgotten to bring mine. I missed it already. There was a text from Cara.

You're mad, you crazy things, but I hope you have fun.

'Good, she's not mad, then?'

'I should imagine she's punching the air,' I said. 'You're forgetting she's still young.'

But our daughter wasn't the type of kid who would be facebooking her friends in Cardiff to pile down for a party, which is exactly the kind of thing I would have done in her shoes. Instead, I knew she'd head straight for the kitchen. I could taste those Welsh cakes of hers, too heavy on the cinnamon.

Nerys had been the same once, and I had thought then, as I do now, it had been a cute pastime – sentimental, loyal – but she'd stopped when Cara had started school, when Cara had been palmed off with a teacher for the day. Palmed off? Sometimes my wife could be as cold as the mountains.

'Palmed off?'

'What? Look over there. Do you think sheep get cold? Do you think they should wear leg warmers?' She watched them, her eyes crusted with sleep, her eyelids flickering with jet-lag. 'Goddamn,' she said, 'do you remember those purple ones I used to wear to yoga?'

'Not one of your better ideas,' I said.

'And look how the sheep blend in to the mountains. It's like nature's deliberately roughed them up.'

'?'

'Nature's made them the colour of Welsh stone.'

For Nerys, life had a special kind of magic. She believed in guardian angels, fate, divining the future. She had a creative heart, my wife, and I wondered if she'd always been plotting a stellar career. I twisted around to retrieve my notebook. *Jesus, woman! You left me, just like that, you cold-hearted woman, you crazy-mad bitch.*

The weirdest part of all this, the source of endless frustration, was I'd just about manage to forget her and she'd appear in my head. The dream was always the same. She walked towards me, her bare feet padding the grass. She kept her arms crossed against her chest and her frown heavy. I tell you, dreams know. There's only so much a man can repress.

My brain whirred. I was thinking again and this was all to the good. I risked a pat on my wife's knee, but she pushed my hand away.

Mind you, she always appeared to like me, a man can tell. The clues were there, you just had to spot them. There was her sly smile, all the more appealing for its lack of fullness. There was her tea chest of seeds waiting to be planted, an investment in us. There was her gift of Cara, our shambolic, crazy daughter, which... okay... was my doing as much as hers. She couldn't take all the credit.

My dreams spoke to me. They gave me a shake and told me what I didn't want to hear. I've always said you can hide away in your sleep but you can't hide from your dreams. They shout in your head: *we will come and find you, we will remind you what she looked like, tasted like. We won't let you forget a single fleshy inch of that mad-crazy bitch.*

So, last night I'd experienced such a dream. Perhaps this had been the dream that put this whole idea in my head in the first place. There'd been rape fields, seas of neon yellow – north Bucks, Warwickshire, Bedfordshire? No matter. The point is I had *company*. There had been a presence with me.

I looked down. My wife's foot was pressed so hard on the accelerator, I saw blue veins around her insteps. They appeared to be pulsing.

'Careful!' I said. 'You'll overheat the engine.'

'In this thing? Are you crazy?'

Finally, we relaxed into silence, and I sat back, wide awake but dizzy. Nerys tapped the wheel. We were once again on the flat and this pleased me. I liked the flat, we could cruise along in second, let the engine breathe. I didn't have to worry if the engine could take the upward haul. We nigh-on glided on the tarmac. I looked back at the mountains. They were no longer the boss of us.

'But anyhow,' she said, 'I've been thinking. Students do this sort of thing. Maybe pensioners milking their last gasp. But we're still a way off that, aren't we?'

'Good.'

'But we're not young either, are we, Duff? Because there's a point. You know when that is, don't you? Forty-two. That's when it happens.'

'Come again?'

She looked at me in a way that told me I knew nothing. Only Nerys had the power.

'In astrological terms, that's middle age – right? And that's just around the corner. For both of us.'

But I wasn't so enamoured with this conversation, this half-cooked mumbo-jumbo. She should have known better than to lay that new-age schtick on me. *Once* she – oh, this is good! She offered to have my chart drawn up as a birthday present. *You're so Venus in Capricorn. Your attitude, it's so repressed. So Venus in –*

'Duff?'

'Hmm?'

'Our soundtrack: what'll be ours, then?'

'Our soundtrack?'

'REM? Talking Heads? The Ramones?' She turned to me. 'Will we download some when we get to York?'

'Ay, well, if we're hurtling to England,' I said, 'a little Americana will go down a treat.'

This is what I missed: a companion with my exact same tastes. Hearing Nerys speak like this, I was fired with love again. I thought of Angharad back in Betwys. Angharad with her severe smile and her zipped-tight purse. There was no comparison. *Dear Angharad, dear deserted Angharad, if only you were the clone of Nerys, I wouldn't have to do what I planned on doing. I wouldn't have to send you away.*

'Wind the window down, will you?' I asked my wife.

'Already?'

'To do this properly, I want the wind blasting my face, like in that film.'

'Which one?'

'You know, Brad Pitt flouncing in the cowboy hat. I'll be an honorary Thelma to your Louise.'

Nerys laughed. Her bangles rattled over the bumps. We trailed a red post van that forced us to slow. Mud flew off our wheels, roughing up the windscreen. My wife eased her foot off the pedal. Quickly, I made some notes. *Ah, I missed your gurgling laughter, taking me through unmarked doors to the secret world of galleries. And your mad ideas! Christ! Do you happen to remember the Pup's Vacation Home? Insane. So, you thought you could leave, just like that, and I –*

But the road ahead was bumpy. I stopped and glanced at my wife who had her mind elsewhere.

'Can I make a suggestion?'

'Go ahead,' I said.

'On the plane, I read about a new boutique hotel opened in Harrogate. Maybe we can stay there?'

I frowned. I had nothing against Harrogate, but this was out of the question. Nerys looked at me, beaten. Damn, I hated that I could make her frown like that. This was the power I'd forgotten I had. Welcome back, old friend.

'I'm sure it's fine,' I said, 'but no, this will derail everything.'

I smiled at her, long and heart-felt. We were as we used to be, students again, fresh-eyed with future plans.

I remembered our first trip together to London from Aberdeen. From the train, we picked out the cities that intrigued us. I chose Berwick for the flat caps and whippets. Nerys chose Durham and York, orderly and aspirational – typical Nerys. Nonetheless, it was to these places I was determined I would take her.

'No, a grabbed sandwich is not what I had in mind at all,' I said. 'I want to navigate the walls, browse the little sweet shops.'

'Oh.'

'I want to drag you down Whip-Ma-Whop-Ma-Gate by your *hair*. I want to taste that soothing, creamy ale.'

Damn it, I would even visit a gallery if that's what she wanted.

'I need comfort, honey – sometimes. Because if it's money you're worried about, don't. I'll take care of that.'

But hearing this from her lips made my heart dip. She was showing off and there would be no life in a hotel like that – not the type of life I was after. I wanted the authentic northern experience in all its shabby glory. There was no way I was going to wade in with the slick types up from London.

'I'm serious,' I said. 'And you're forgetting it's a Saturday – the weekend. We'll never find a room.'

We arrived in York in the evening. The moon hung low, bluing our path. We edged into the traffic, bumper-to-bumper. I took in the cobbled paving; the almost-circle wall and its ancient ways; the sombre, terraced houses.

In Marygate, by the Museum Gardens, we parked up, facing the muddy river. I breathed in deep. Sluggishly, I spied a neat little pub a few rows down. A faint smell of hops flooded the van and I hauled myself out. To me, Yorkshire was another country. It could hold its own, nicely.

'Wait, hold on, I'll Google some numbers,' Nerys said.

'No you won't. How do you think people used to manage? Wait here a minute, I'll knock on some doors.'

The pub I entered was no bigger than my front room. A brass lion roared at me from the mantelpiece. I could smell the beer stains, the smoky curtains – perfection. My mouth watered to see the ales, only a handful I'd seen the like of in Swansea. So with a handful of change, I bought one, a take-out bottle, green and long. The barmaid's thumb directed me outside to the privy. There, I found myself shivering in a square foot of yard. I unzipped my fly. Already this was an adventure.

I returned to the barmaid. She was all heavy eyeshadow and eye liner. She told me her friend next door should have a room or two, if I was to ask him nicely. With a hard-mouthed smirk she nodded to the campervan outside, blocking the light. Her laugh was deep and gravelly, the real deal.

Outside, Nerys slammed the door and together we rang a doorbell. A pensioner, a brown cardigan and weighty jowls, guided us through. We waited. Pictures of Churchill and Princess Anne darkened the walls. We heard a voice, a woman complaining of underwear left to dry on the radiator.

'Well, this is friendly,' Nerys said. 'Shall we go?'

But I failed to see the big deal with accommodation. As long as there was a bed and clean towels, I was happy.

'Well, I guess we'll be out later,' Nerys conceded. 'It's just somewhere to crash – right?'

The cardigan returned. His shoulders were hunched forward, like a lifetime of watching his wife change the sheets had taken its toll. He told us he had one room remaining: the honeymoon suite. Alarm bells clanged in my ears. I could barely take the excitement. What the *hell* would a honeymoon suite consist of in a place like this?

'But you don't understand, we're not a couple,' Nerys said. And, at this, I was wounded afresh. I trailed behind the cardigan and my wife, through the back yard to an out-house, a kind of granny annexe. Cautiously, I opened the door. The man left and we stepped inside. What we saw before us defied all we had come to understood about life, the universe and everything. At the foot of the bed was a collection of smiling gnomes. Nerys swivelled one in the light, admiring its blank smile.

'Duff, it's twinkling its eyes at me. And look, this one has an ear missing.'

My wife belly-flopped on the bed, scanning her head left, then right. There were fairies perched on the bedside table and angels dangling from the bedpost. Optimistically, I poked my head round the door of the *en suite*. My brain whirred and my heart flicked around inside my chest. This was *exactly* the type of experience I was after. All fodder for my journal and my drug-addled mind. Nerys looked at me.

'What is it? What can you see?'

'It's an avocado suite,' I said. 'And the shower has disabled rails.'

She eyed me defeated, like a stunned doe.

'Gnomes,' she said. 'Duff, there are gnomes in a bedroom. Now, I've – how will we – this is something but – '

'Something else,' I said.

'It's far-out, that's what it is.'

I hadn't heard this expression for a while, but it beat her usual Americanisms. So, I asked her to budge up. I took my trousers off, left my pants on and I opened my notebook to the sound of gentle snoring. *Through sad eyes, I watched you bend over the cold, yellow crocuses. I watched the rain soak your skin, your eyelashes, your shoes. I noticed the skin on the tips of your fingers, like tiny walnuts. Swinging left, then right, your skirt floated in the breeze. In the kitchen, I rubbed you dry. Up and down, up, down. Your face was blank, but my heart was bursting. Then, under a cruel sun…you left me and you were gone.*

I remembered the envelopes that had started to fall through the letterbox with steady regularity. They had been windowed and brown, official-looking. Just tax matters, she told me. There were hand-written envelopes too. Neat handwriting. A pen pal, she'd told me. Kim, she'd said, Kim in Santa Fe. *Now Duff, I've told you before, why don't you listen to me? We were in school together. We've been back in touch.*

Kim had recently divorced, she told me. *Having a pen pal is a harmless pastime, Duff, you can't argue with that.* But she'd breathed her hot lies all over my face.

So, Kim? Which one were you? Back then, did you wear glasses? Were you the one all the boys hated but the girls liked because you didn't pose a threat? I –

I slipped the blue lid back on my biro. Kim had been a fiction, there was no doubt, but back then I wanted her to be real. If I'd thought to, I could have read these letters while Nerys was out shopping. I would have known for sure.

My eyes drooped and I watched my wife sleeping under the garish, pink lightshade. There was a wispy golden glow to her arms and legs. Rembrandt had painted people with a golden glow, I knew that much. I watched her sleep with her mouth open and innocent. But I was sad for all the time that had passed, the times I'd wanted her, begged for her body to fill the empty space between my body and the cold wall.

Time had ticked away and so had my libido. I couldn't have allowed anyone else, not even Angharad, to spend the whole night with me, not with Cara in the next room, and not when my memories were as strong as they were. I had come to accept I was middle-aged.

After my coma-like nap, I was treated to a tap on my arm, gentle at first. I blinked. The big numbers on the clock flashed their warning. It was after nine. My eyes were foggy and dull. I watched her switch on the bedroom lamp.

My wife's face was transformed, her cheeks glowing, her lips stained. She wore a long dress with flowers, just the type of frock a woman should wear. Her heels were high and red. Taller, prouder, that was how she looked to me. She smelt like Nerys: the woman who used to be mine. She smelt earthy and unmistakably her. I breathed her in. As she wafted around me, slipping on her shoes, I smiled. I could still remember what it was like to spoon her. I could still remember the haphazard rhythm of her belly.

I used to love to hear Nerys breathe. Facing me, facing the wall, she did all kinds of manoeuvres. Nerys had been a biter. She'd liked to clamp me between her legs and sink her teeth into my shoulders. They were tiny teeth but they were sharp.

So, together, we headed through the house. We passed the brown cardigan sipping tea at his table. He didn't even look up – yes, yes fine, couldn't want for better, no, no perfect – and we stepped onto the cold street.

In Bootham, we found a cramped cellar with a square dance floor. There was a make-shift bar. We grabbed a stool each and sat at a high table. Behind the bar, a woman in black and white stripes reached a glass up to the optics. I wondered what it would be like to taste her fuchsia lipstick. It was a young crowd: students, the drunk and the hopeless. It smelt of perfume and damp clothes.

With my tongue still dry and hot, I sipped red wine to music that crashed and skiffed, chafed and spat. What I needed was to wake up and soon.

'Terrible. Not the type of thing I was after at all,' I said. 'Shall we dance?'

Nerys looked around her. I caught her jealously eyeing the barmaid.

'Are you serious, hon? Nobody else is dancing – right?'

But that was the point. This was my plan. I had to force myself out of myself a little. If I could be seen to do what others in the human race enjoyed, my wife would remember how much she had wanted me back then. It had been so long but I was certain her feelings could be resurrected.

'And while we're at it,' I said, 'you can tell me all about it.'

'Tell you?'

'All about Santa Fe and life over there.'

On the flashing tiles – yellow, red, red, yellow – Nerys danced harder than I'd ever seen her do. She was a dervish, all clucking arms and swivelling hip-bones. I couldn't match her, but I was surprised by how much her new lust for life was contagious. With a heaving chest, I sped up. I shook my gangly legs and moved around the dance floor with her. What the hell did it matter? Playing the fool was better than having no fun at all.

'You know all this is a false high, don't you?' Nerys said. 'Trauma can do this to a man.'

'Maybe,' I said.

The music slowed to a tinny wail. My wife stopped, turned her back on me and stepped away. I was alone again and I watched her at the bar. She slipped a note to the fuchsia lipstick in exchange for two, short drinks. I waited for her at the table.

'So, what's your poison?' she asked. 'A tequila or a rum and coke?'

'Looks expensive,' I said.

'Honestly, it's my shout. So, come on, which one?'

I sipped the rum and coke; it tasted like warm aluminium. Nerys looked around her, taking in the noisy scene we were now too old to enjoy. Her restless eyes darted around. It was a process, how Nerys behaved in a public space. She did this, she liked to make sure she was sparkiest, the prettiest catch in the room. Of course, there were other girls mulling around – younger, trendier, but you had to admire my wife's gall.

'So are you inspired?' she asked me. 'You're doing a Kerouac already? What have you got there?'

She glanced at my jeans pockets and reached her hand across. Playfully, I slapped her wrist away. I had written very little was the honest answer, certainly nothing I could share with my wife. But she pleaded with her almond eyes until I crumbled. From my blazer pocket, I pulled a fistful of Nectar receipts. We looked at the faint print shot through with my scrawl.

'Can I take a closer look?'

'Go ahead,' I said.

She picked one, like pulling a raffle ticket.

'Let me – ah, I see you're having trouble pinning down the sun. Shall I help you? It glows, Duff, the sun, it glows. At least I've always thought so.'

She leaned in closer and I returned her sarcastic smile. Her lips looked slimy and I wanted to taste them, aware this was desire I was experiencing. I wanted to hold on to the feeling in fear it would fade. She reached her hand forward. Deftly, she pulled my notebook from my pocket. I snatched it back. Her shoulder straps slipped down her arm.

'Enough Nerys,' I said. 'A man must have his secrets.'

I glanced around me. I saw pale limbs meshing into each other. Others were having fun, so why weren't we? My wife looked around the room for something, someone better – anyone.

Having spent the night with my wife's toes inches from my nose, I woke a little crotchety. My back was stiff. My eyes were sore from last night's smoke machine. With my chest wheezing and whistling its discomfort, I looked down past my feet. The gnomes were there, of course, aloof in the rude, morning light.

I reached across for a biscuit and placed one on my tongue; it was light and sugary and melted on impact. From the quiet, comfort of my bed, I listened to the quiet chirrups of the birds in the yard, the slow drip-drip of water in the gutter. I breathed in long and deep.

The air was busy with the stench of fried eggs and the smell offended me. I checked my watch and wondered where my wife could be. At a loss, I picked up my pen. *YOU: the cold-hearted, out-for-herself bitch. I'd been numbed when you left me, split sideways, left for dead. Don't think I forget so easily. Your dungarees; plaits; eyelashes; feet, bare; hands, scratched; toes, stubbed; lips, drying in the wind; deep baths; quick showers; coal tar soap. Coal tar soap. Coal tar SOAP.* Think man, think. Try to recall a simpler time when your parents were still alive and you were safe. It was true: my parents had liked Nerys, but Nerys had been scared of my mother, the fierce matron in male brogues. To Nerys, my mother had been the woman with the Medusa gaze.

I recalled the first time I had taken her home to meet my parents. The snow had come early. Nerys had pressed her nose up to the window. The night's heavy snowstorm had transformed the garden. Outside, Nerys crunched her feet alongside the prints left by the night animals. They had been the work of foxes, or badgers, or birds. We watched kids in woolly hats sliding down a hill on cheap plastic. Up and down they went, like a human conveyer belt.

Inside, my father was all-out to impress in his best gingham shirt. He fussed round the kitchen. 'Watch out, girl, you'll catch your death in that flimsy number. Here, have this towel.' He'd watched her rub herself dry, a beat too long. Medusa lifted her eyes above her paper. She turned the pages without taking in a word.

'Honey?' Nerys stood before me, holding a scrunched napkin in her hand. Crumbs of pastry dotted her blouse. 'You're too late. You should have got up sooner.'

I rose and pulled on my trousers. She couldn't have woken me? That would have killed her.

She moved quickly. I didn't even have time to tie the laces of my trainers. Sleepily, I followed her through the main house and back to the van, tripping over my laces as I went. The cardigan was nowhere to be seen.

'The murky bowl next,' I said, trying to sound casual, but bent double with hunger.

'Honestly, Duff, did you not change your trousers? We need to think of these things in here.'

Patiently, I ignored this. I pulled out the road map. My gut creaked louder than my lungs. Nerys leaned back and rested her elbow on the window ledge. Before long, I snapped at her to take the A-road.

'Here,' she said. 'I found a bag of crisps in my bag. Your favourite. Prawn cocktail.'

I grabbed them and munched them down, like a pregnant woman hungry for coal. This is what life was like with Nerys by my side: crisps for breakfast. Some fast living.

'Goddamn it,' she said. 'I have my foot down all the way but we're still only doing forty. Crazy.'

Calm again, I gazed at passing cows. I wondered what they made of this man passing by in a campervan. They might see a relaxed holidaymaker, his hands clasped tight above his head. They might see a man on the edge with his best years behind him and only divorce and death to look forward to. They might see a man desperate to reconnect with the only woman he's ever loved.

Still, I couldn't deny my wife's choice of words – Goddamn, Crazy, Right – were starting to rankle. She was an All-American femme fatale these days, too quick to surrender to those Trans-Atlantic ways. The problem with Nerys was she made you see what she wanted you to see. I blinked and the cows blinked back. I narrowed my eyes and pictured them wearing back-to-front caps. They wore long, gold chains and paisley bandanas. They became her students in Santa Fe, speaking all manner of nonsense.

'Wales where? Ah, Wales, England, right?'

'What?' She gripped the wheel hard. 'Please Duff, a hotel tonight.'

'No.'

'You're being surly, selfish again.'

I was? I was and I thought of a way I could cheer her up

without resorting to compromise. I suggested a game. She sat up straight and ready to begin.

'Hide and seek?'

Ah, the bitter-sweet irony.

'No. We'll make words from number plates,' I said, 'and the longer the better, like we used to. There! RKG: Raking. Wrecking. Reckoning.'

'Oh, nice. CRT: Crust. Carrot. Secrets.'

Even nicer. My wife could be so much more than a pretty face. Nerys was clever in a way that was *interesting*. Not for her the studied smartness mined from reading books. No, my wife was a different kind of smart: she was a freethinker, a loose cannon, an *innovator*. I'd have to ask her to show me some of those designs of hers, but I wondered about life back at the ranch. Cara wasn't happy.

Cara had been a good kid once, one of the easy ones. Before Nerys had left, the farm had been everything to her. I remembered those days as clearly as if they were last month. Her favourite hobby had been to grab a handful of chicken feed. She'd watch it fall through her fingers, like rain. She'd sprinkle some through the wire. The youngest chicken, Pepper, pecked and jerked. His yellow beak jutted from a wrinkled, puce ring, and she'd scoop him up and jiggle him. It was amazing to her how his head stayed still. I had taught her this. I had my uses.

Nerys. Did she miss those days as much as me? I hadn't realised then, but those days when Cara was small were the happiest of my life. They weren't to last. I wondered if Nerys had known how much I'd suffered, whether she would have cared. Because Nerys had faded, turned to grey, that was the worst of it.

I pulled out my notebook and glanced across to see my wife smiling blankly at the road ahead. *I'd taken to wandering alone, under a watching moon. The bats swung past in the dark as I went...* Optimistically, I'd convinced myself I had been all my wife had wanted. Duff Boyd had been the one who set her up. Duff Boyd had carried the load, bought her all she needed. In my own head, I'd been her whole world. But it had been stifling on the farm, according to Nerys.

Okay, so I'd been a coward, no better than the cockerels, but what of it? Because we're all chickens when it comes to the ones we love. Nerys, of all people would know about that. I should have begged her to come back, wrote a letter, lengthy and pleading. I should have sent her the airfare for good measure. *Drop everything, come back now, don't be silly – good game.* But I didn't, I was a fool. How to solve a problem like Nerys? My wife glared at me, wondering why I was smiling.

'Simple chap, isn't he?' I said. 'Not much up there?'

'Who?'

'Daryl, Cara's boyfriend.'

Nerys tapped her wrists on the wheel. My water spilled. I grabbed a tissue from the glove compartment and mopped myself. Without my noticing, we had slipped onto the motorway. The straight, monochrome lines dulled my senses.

I glanced up. The sky was a cold blue. The clouds were mellow and frothy.

'What do you think Durham is like, Duff? Because it looked beautiful from the train that time.'

She looked shyly at me to remember that day. I smiled. My wife could say the right thing at exactly the right moment. Talking to Nerys was a miracle in itself – what's more, the past became an exciting place, no longer a torment.

'Have another,' she said and handed me a tissue from her pack.

'Ah, I imagine there's a fair few places selling chips – chips swimming in beef fat,' I said. 'Plenty of old-timers knocking back the ale.'

She turned to me.

'What else?'

There was an innocence in her look that made me want to drape my arm around her. But I didn't touch her. I knew not to push.

'A chocolate-coloured river,' I said. 'Maybe a Michelin up in the hills. But aren't towns much of a muchness these days? They call them clone towns for a reason.'

She leaned back and thought for a moment.

'Not Durham, surely?'

Ah. My wife wanted to believe Durham was a special place and I didn't want to quash her illusions. She was tired of America, I was sure. She was riddled with regret for the life she'd left behind. She missed the good life, the cobbled streets, without a doubt.

We arrived in Durham an hour before dusk. The Murky Bowl looked tired in the moonlight. A river of caramel spilled through the middle. To me, the place was a black valley, a special, hard place, but there was something about being down so low that sunk me. It was unfamiliar and gloomy, not the town of my dreams. Nonetheless, I made out I was happy for Nerys's sake.

We settled in our new resting hole, all dazzling pink chintz and thundering pipes. Reclining on the bed, I waited for her to finish up in the bathroom. I took time out for my thoughts and grappled with the pillows. They were flat and under-fibred. Damn. I missed my duck-hair ones. All my home comforts.

To cheer myself, I conjured the time we first saw Durham from the train. I'd *wanted* to get Nerys pregnant that night in London. That had been my one thought in the fug. I wondered had she known that about me, that I'd wanted her baby that night. Ay, there'd been no doubt.

I'd stroked her cheek. She'd jumped up and grabbed a spare cushion from the top of wardrobe. She threw it at me. Dancing naked on the bed, she flashed a triangle of red hair down there. She'd revelled in my watching her, swelling like someone important, an empress. Later, I'd lapped her up, every hair-sprouting follicle.

With a crash, Nerys swung open the bathroom door. She wore a short, pencil skirt and her white cotton blouse was open down to the top of her red bra. Her eyebrows were dark, and pronounced. If she wore glasses, she'd look ready to take a letter. Her legs were brown and streaky, the mild colour of turmeric. I wondered what the hell she had in that make-up sack of hers.

We headed out by foot, taking our time, mooching up steep roads and back down again. We passed charcoal houses and even blacker churches. The air dribbled with the smell of beef fat. Finally, we found the creamy pint I'd been pining for. The pub was small and lively. There was a jukebox, varnished floorboards and men shooting pool. We settled at a round table near the door. Nerys leaned in.

'You know what it is you need?'

There was the pleasing smell of juniper on her breath.

'Oh ay?'

'A little taste of the old times, how it used to be.'

'Naughty, cryptic. Tell me more,' I said.

'So, I reckon what we should do is get drunk, absolutely plastered, like we used to do. What's the worst – ?'

'Behave like teenagers?'

'Exactly like teenagers. I could drink you under the table anytime.'

She twirled the tips of her hair.

'Could not,' I said.

'Could so. If last night's anything to go by. Honestly Duff, that was pathetic.'

'Ha,' I said. 'Anyway, you Americans, aren't you all about health these days?'

Nerys smirked.

'Well, you can take the girl out of Wales.'

But I could see my wife was restless. She smoothed her skirt down. I watched her wiggle to the bar – a *kind* of wiggle.

She spoke with a pout, like she was rolling gold around her tongue. She returned with a tray, carrying neat whiskeys and tequila slammers.

'No, Duff. Tequila first.'

'But that's the chaser?'

'No, I need that salty taste now.'

I watched her down hers and I smiled. Her face tightened and she shivered.

'You know what I call it?'

'Tell me,' I said.

'It's legal cocaine, that's what it is – a natural high.'

She watched me down my whisky.

'Now, Duff, you were supposed to neck the tequila first.'

'In for a penny,' I said.

She licked the rim of her glass, hungry for more.

'An ouzo next? A sambuca?'

'A what? No, how about a glass of Benedictine?' I suggested, relaxing into her game.

'A who? Can you see it on the shelves?'

We got up and I showed her.

'There. Top shelf.'

Using a tea towel, the noisome-haired barman dusted it off. I could smell stale beer coming from his Guinness T-shirt. We watched him study the label.

'You see,' I said. 'A drink of Kings. One that hasn't been touched – ever. I didn't actually think they'd have it.'

My wife swung around to face me. I watched the arch of her back cup the bar. She looked pleasing and shapely, just as I remembered.

'You wanna know something else, hon?' she asked.

I did want to know, as it happened, of course I did.

'You've still got it.'

'Pardon?'

'Your hair, you still have it. You're not receding yet.'

Ah, but that was where she was wrong. I smiled at her. With the alcohol flushing through me she was radiant, she was beautiful. Her silky cheeks shone. Her grin crackled confidence. She was the type of woman who could do so much better.

'Wanna know something else?' I said.

'Shoot!'

'I prefer you natural. Tell me, why do you wear all that?'

It was hard to ignore the surplus beige gunk gathering around the corners of her mouth. I didn't understand why she wanted to hide her natural beauty.

'Why go bare at my age? Are you crazy?'

I shrugged. She leaned in closer and patted my behind. I checked my watch, it was after nine.

In the early days of our relationship, Nerys had fascinated me. Back in my digs, with my trousers down to my knees, I couldn't shake the thought of her. I'd stroked myself in the lamplight until my hand became her hand. My fascination soon turned to obsession.

'Look, up there,' she said, pointing outside. 'The sky's cleared. So here's what we should do: we'll stop off at the off-licence on the way home. There's still time. It's not ten yet. Let's get a bottle of bubbly. Take it to bed if you like. We can flick our way through the sports channels.'

Aha. This was *her* trump card. Canny.

'And the catch?'

'The catch is…well, you'll see.'

Sat on the toilet, I rubbed the newly grown bristles on my chin. I was still floating from the morphine pills. It was a bitter kind of high. My lips were dry, my stomach was tight. I listened. Sirens passed on the street below, loud and piercing. My wife was safely out of sight but I heard her shouts. She told me Rangers scored a goal against Celtic, an easy one, a fluke.

I found Nerys flopped on the bed, her bottom facing up, sipping champagne through a straw. I took the armchair under the television. There was an almighty roar. I wondered what was going on above my head – a missed goal? Nerys looked a little crazy, flame-eyed and drunken, smiling to herself. She shot up and pulled me down on top of her.

'Not there. Now, not there, you know what – '

'You're still mine, hon, go on, admit it,' she said. 'I still have a hold on you.'

'What do you mean, you crazy bitch? You never left me. I'm still up here.' I tapped her head. 'Go on, admit it.'

But she didn't answer. Instead, she yanked her top to one side and I saw a flash of red bra. She clamped me to her and we were skin on skin. Hers was warm and damp. Mine was dry and in need of the moisture. She smelt of sex, love and hot, baked bread.

'Do the pussy thing,' I said. 'Like you used to.' And I

watched her blow her lips, once, twice, three times. 'Jesus, woman. Tell me, what the hell happened to us?'

But no good would come of hearing her speak. Talk was for the other times when we weren't together in bed. I was falling, clamped in those great thighs of hers. Her mouth was soft and steamy-wet, like two half-moons – two half-moons I could finally taste.

In the morning, I rolled over and faced her. Her pores spewed sour, stale ethanol. I'd blown it, I thought, the whole trip, the whole sorry she-bang.

But back in London that time, I'd had my way with her as any sane man would – what's more I'd had my wish. Eight months and nineteen days later, Cara was born. I took a photo of my wife holding a perfect, slimy baby. My wife bloomed with a strange, fertile puffiness to her cheeks. I still cherish the faded Polaroid. She is suspended forever in time, creased forward, laughing. A long, long time back.

Santa Fe, Santa Fe, Santa Fe, what is there to do all day? America. America. America, you came along and swallowed her. Santa Fe had taken her away from me, but it sounded like a nutso place. Nothing but a Butlins for washed-up hippies, balls-deep in debt to the crack wolves. No place to call home. I decided what I needed was to take care of Nerys. I could show her how life could really be. *So, you thought I was to blame? Shame on you for thinking that. It's true: I've been distant, selfish – if you insist – but the smallholding was for the three of us. No, too convenient of you to use "business" as an excuse.*

More than anything, it was the safety I missed, the lifestyle. When you're married, you can get away with anything – and I mean *anything*. Nerys enjoyed the rhythm of daily life too.

Women like her, when they're safe, they kick back a bit, you know? They wear off-white pants. They waddle around in grey vests and kick used socks around the floor. They lick the plate – the greedy cats! What you do is you meld into the comfort. You punch at your weight.

I wait for her, wind my window down and sniff the muddy grass. There was a point when I'd taken a wrong turn, I was sure. I wasn't the type of man to react unreasonably, the type of man to rise to her tantrums. I didn't close off when she made simple, unnecessary demands. I didn't sleep around. Well, not much.

I coughed and stared at the Italian restaurant opposite. Nerys carefully looked both ways before crossing at the zebra. Those thighs of her, they could crack the toughest hazelnuts.

Nerys climbed back in and put her foot down. Soon we found ourselves lost in the green. I took her in. My wife looked young and sleepy, newly born. It was still morning. Her eyes were hazy and not yet focussed. This endeared me to her, made me want to protect her.

Nerys told me she would like a chance to talk properly this time, a heart-to-heart in the warm light of day. She suggested a pub lunch in Berwick-upon-Tweed. I half-listened, for once happy to oblige.

I liked Berwick. The aqueduct looked like a giant comb stretched across the water. There were terracotta roofs on whitewashed buildings. The place was clouded in industrial vapour. There was a cooling, northern breeze.

On the edge of town, Nerys pointed to a stone pub on the crest of the hill. My stomach rumbled, painfully so. I dropped my smile.

'You know, all this excitement,' she said, 'and it hadn't occurred to me, you could have slept in here.'

'Not together, then?'

'Steady on now,' she said. 'Besides, look – no, there, see? No, that's it – under that blanket.'

'?'

'I've gone and brought a tent with me.'

Ah, yes, that was typical Nerys. Secretive, but practical.

Inside the pub we tuned in and out of unfamiliar voices. We watched grown men huddle over mash and meat pies. This, to me, was the proper North Country: strangers, werewolves, freaks, this is what we were now, and it pleased me. We sat down, and placed our orders. With my hunger growing, I looked out across the fields. A gardener in an open shirt gave me the finger. I scowled back. At the bar, a hand twirled a towel inside a pint glass.

'Do you not find this strange?' Nerys said. 'Goddamn England's not as friendly as I remember.'

'Ay, well, you've been gone a while, babe.'

The barmaid brought our food. She looked my wife up and down with a sprinkling of envy. Discreetly, I checked my notebook. There was to be a full moon later. Good, it might inspire me. I watched Nerys spear a potato. She was thinking again, I could tell.

'Duff, I suppose I'd better tell you now. I'm not sure about this. It's all changed. What do you think? It doesn't feel right, does it? Not now, not after last night.'

'What?'

Nerys shook her head. I heard her feet tapping under the table.

'Look hon, I know. But when you suggested all this business, I was pleased because I've thought of it often.'

'In Santa Fe?'

'I guess, but it's not the same now, is it? Too much has changed. We've run out of gas.'

My wife ate slowly, chewing every morsel. Suddenly, I wasn't hungry.

'What do you mean?' I asked. 'The van's fine and there's plenty of gas in the back.'

'I'm not talking about the petrol,' she said. 'It's too late for us now. Think about it, honey, please, for the sake of our sanity. If we carry on, we'll just go deeper. No, don't look at me like that. Try to understand. Aberdeen will never lose its shine. It never could. It's all up here – tap tap – so do me a favour, let's leave it there, okay?'

If I held my breath in the silence, I could just about hear my bones creak. I studied my long arms, twisting them clockwise, then back again. They were the same arms, but they were strangely powerless.

'But why? How can you just change your mind like this?'

She shrugged.

'A girl has the right to, doesn't she? It was only a temporary high, all this. A pipe dream. The other night on the dance floor we said as much ourselves.'

We had said this, I hadn't forgotten, these exact words were spoken, but I wasn't ready to back down.

'Look, the view changes from here,' I said. 'Going back down south it's all grey roads and motorway. The further up we go, the better it gets, *you* know that.'

But I knew I'd have to conjure more appealing images.

'It's a beaut up there. Rambling, wild. You love that stretch. The purple heather. The thistles and clear water. All empty beaches. Remember that time?'

She rubbed sweet-smelling cream into her hands.

'True,' she said, looking brighter, at least.

'And if it'll make you happy,' I said. 'If you don't want a repeat of last night, I'll sleep in the van.'

'Well I – you promise you will? You won't do that puppy-eyed schtick? Because I won't fall for it, Duff. You know me.'

'Yes,' I said. 'I know you well. Whatever it takes.'

With her face neutral again, my wife thanked me. Once more I'd won time to play with. Because play was what we needed. I knew love would die without it. If we could just make our way up to the bleak Northumberland coast, she would melt at its magnificence. It would be perfect and simple. We would dive in streams and scoff at the locals, eat local food and drown in their ales. The whole point of travel was to try new things. Moreover, it was down to me to prove she could trust me. We finished our roasts in silence. Lightly, she flicked my arm.

'You know, when we were together, I could tell when you were far away.'

'How so?'

'I imagined spinning coins in your head, until they wobbled and stopped.'

'Every time?'

'No, not every time,' she said.

Nerys swivelled her finger in a tiny pot. She dotted glittery gunk on her lips.

'Can I ask you something?'

'Sure,' I said. 'What is it?'

'When it comes down to it, you're wobbling a bit, aren't you? We both are, aren't we?'

'Ay,' I said. 'I do believe we are.'

I wondered about my wife at times. She'd looked sure enough last night under the weight of me, flirty and in control.

Nerys smiled wide and sincere. I studied her face, fresh and pretty. In the orangey light, she didn't look like my wife at all: she looked like somebody else's wife, the kind of wife who could attract guys with the smart money.

'Another drink?'

'Just the one, then,' she said. 'Can't harm, I guess.'

'BRB,' I said.

At the bar, I pulled out my wallet and scrambled around for sufficient change. My card was my only currency, so I handed it over. Declined. I thought about my wife's lovers over in Santa Fe. Rupert and Taryn and Sabina, the lesbian.

But I grinned to think of Nerys trying her best to be different. She wouldn't have lasted long batting for the other side.

Nerys sidled up beside me. She tapped my arm.

'No, on second thoughts, you better hold that drink. I think we'd better get moving.'

Too much, too soon. They say that, don't they? Nerys and me had married young. Back then, I hadn't known the full weight of my responsibilities. I'd heard about marriage. I knew any sane man would want a home and a wife and kids, but had I thought how that could work? Of course not. Nonetheless, I was older and calmer these days, ready and willing to change. She just needed to give me time.

I'd revised my opinion of Berwick-upon-Tweed. It hadn't been the cosy place of our dreams. It had been a dull little town, all sleepy lanes and run-down dealerships. We'd ticked off the last of our choices. I wondered had we peaked too soon? Idly, I flicked through the tunes on my wife's iPod. Nerys had eclectic tastes, but... Celine Dion? Katy Perry? The Spinners? She handed me another iPod, a bigger one – better, yes, but still, no. The trouble with Nerys was she was too easily influenced.

'I was thinking,' I said. 'You remember that time on the train?'

Nerys looked at me. I detected a glint of sympathy.

'Are we back to this again?'

'You took a swig of my ale, remember? You slid your

hands down there to *the place.* I had to use my duffel coat to y'know – '

She tapped the heels of her palms on the wheel, happy to remember.

'We were young though, weren't we? And do you remember the old woman?'

'Knitting the chocolate squares? Ay, she knew what you were up to, didn't she, you naughty minx. Didn't stop you though, did it? You carried on talking – questions, questions. You asked if I wanted to go there with you.'

'Where?'

My wife put her foot down. We were alone on the narrow road, following the line of a low, stone wall. We passed a white cottage with a red tin roof.

'Have you forgotten?' I asked, trying to sound casual but my eagerness frothed in my chest.

'Berwick,' I said. 'Berwick-upon-Tweed.'

'Did I? That's funny, what possessed me?'

But I knew she had said exactly those words. My wife looked at me.

'It stank of tobacco in that carriage, didn't it?' she said. 'That was the way back then.'

So, I indulged in our sweet memory. The window had been filthy, scratched and yellowing. Nerys had stroked me down there – down there where my frustration grew – grew to the size of a zeppelin. Silently, I'd answered her. Perhaps we will. Perhaps we will. Perhaps we will.

'Perhaps we will.'

'Come again?'

'Something like that,' I said.

'Honestly, Duff, if we're going ahead with this, you should get the map out. There's a lot of exits around here – so I know when –'

'You want to?'

'Sure. What's the difference? We'll only be back at the farm with you sulking.'

Later, in the dark, we parked up in a field, far from anywhere. The only sign of life was a house, a mile-or-so deep in the shadows. I switched on my pocket torch. Across the way, a sheep dog chased a tractor into the mouth of darkness. I watched the driver hurl a fag butt in the dog's face. The dog circled round and round, undeterred. Before me, caged in the centre of the field, two cows rested, compliant and docile. We set up camp behind a large oak.

From the van, I watched her grapple with the tent pegs. They were bent and as good as useless but she swung a wooden mallet high and nailed them down. When she'd finished, she came over and helped me with my bed. I slid under my blanket and tried to coax her down to my lips.

'Come closer,' I mouthed. 'I can't hear you. No, closer.' Her cheek smelt of warm orchids but tasted like an oil slick. She tucked me in.

'Aren't you going to thank me?' she asked.

'What for?'

'For agreeing to carry on. Indulge this crazy trip of yours.'

I corrected her. 'Of ours.'

'Whatever hon. So? I'm waiting for you to say it.'

My wife was always pushing, forever wanting to be

adored. I didn't want to thank her. Instead, I watched her turn her back on me and leave. With my nose pressed to the van roof, I heard her shout nighty-night up into the trees. The rain pelted hard, inches from my eyes. I wondered how she'd cope out there with only the stars for company. My lungs creaked, affecting my concentration. When I breathed, I wheezed, and I knew it would be hours before I could catch some sleep. With my mind drifting, I remembered a day that haunted me. I thought of it often.

'It's too difficult,' Nerys said. 'Too much has happened – too much.'

I pulled her up from her the table and led her to the window. Around us was chaos – plates waiting to be washed, grime congealing on all surfaces. The kettle whistled.

'Look,' I said. 'Take a good look. This was all your idea.'

For want of anything better to do, the chickens danced in their coop. The black-nosed sheep faced away towards the downcast mountains, fierce in the drizzle. Nerys peered out to the broken bench, wrecked by my own foot. I could be fiery with inanimate objects.

'But the winters, they're too cold. And my feet hurt. My clothes – look at this,' she tugged at her skirt hem. 'Unravelling. I just can't do this, Duff. I try but…'

I blinked away a tear. So, I had been tiresome, selfish, and I had failed to make her life as happy as it could be. But now, with her help I could change. The point of Nerys and me was we were a team. We trod the turf together. I missed not having her around to help me with Cara. I had to cope alone with her juvenile mood swings, her truancy. I tried to be both parents in one imperfect package, but a girl needs her mother.

More than this, I missed not being able to take care of my own wife's needs. I missed the sweet smell of her. Life was pointless without having to do everything with Nerys in mind. *The surplus energy is carried over, but where does it go? Do the waves of energy carry on, without reason or rhyme?*

With sleep a long way off, and with no other option than to do *something*, I read back over my notebook. *Man and wife, mouths tight shut, a Pacific ocean between us. A lifetime of – what? Angharad, tight-fisted Angharad, selfish.* I shifted on the slab and put down my torch. Through the small, rusty window I watched water trickle down the canvas of her tent. It formed a small pool by her closed zip. *She'll be fine, ay. My crazy-mad wife can take care of herself.*

I woke the next morning with a stiff shoulder and a distinct rattle in my chest. My brain processed a humdrum symphony of sounds: sneezing; manic nose-blowing; a spoon clashing against tin. Nerys whistled to herself, a tune I didn't recognise. A Welsh folk tune. Nerys knew them all.

I lay flat on my stomach and took a whack on my inhaler. Like a sedated turtle, I rotated 180 degrees. I spied her through my tiny gash of a window. Lazily, I watched her pull her jumper over her head. I noticed her goose-bumps. Slowly, she mopped her armpits with a wipe. She lay flat on her stomach, preparing for another one of her crazy yoga moves. One of the animal poses. The ground sheet lay under her. I closed my eyes.

I sensed – I sensed several things: our lives were flashing by. We were at the midpoint of our lives, on the cusp of growing old. I had a wife – an estranged wife and a daughter. Both were my responsibility, but they'd scarred me in their own sweet ways. Cara was innocent. Mercifully for her, she had her own life – a life that would stretch beyond the world I could offer her. As for Nerys: Nerys was her own energy wave, freewheeling and infinite. Luckily, I was here to save her.

I looked down to my toes. It was true: my body had failed me, my health had nose-dived, left me broken and bruised. But I also knew soon enough I would bloom. What I needed most of all was an adventure. I heard a voice calling from the wings. The stage director shouts: *don't just stand there, Duff, move your feet. You know what you have to do – what you have to do is keep on moving.*

'Duff? Duff?'

I did the turtle shift again to face the van door. Nerys leaned against the frame.

'I see someone's taking it easy. Don't bust a gut, will you? Look hon, we need to crack on. Don't forget, there's the coast for lunch.'

She whacked her shoe on the door frame. The wet mud was caked on and wouldn't shift. I watched her go. Dizzy, I dressed and heaved my sorry frame into the front.

Ever since I swapped farm life for The Faculty, I couldn't shake the feeling I was headed for a fall. My days were numbered there. I wasn't popular enough; I wasn't a *speaker* – not an all-dancing, all-singing one – hell, not even a competent one. When I rambled on, the students kept their heads down – but why? Had they been drawing my head in the gallows? My nuts under the hammer – what? My notes were under-prepared, panicked lines from a man on the edge. The students knew this, of course, I'd credit them that. My students had a taste for blood. They ate men like me for lunch.

No, if I'd been sharper, more ambitious, I could have made my mark in The Faculty. I could have used my intelligence to wean some serious contacts, not the d-listers I'd settled for. I could have whored myself around the papers and made lots of money.

Nerys climbed in beside me and tapped the wheel. Slowly, we edged out of our illicit field – too slowly for the farmer, as it turned out. A barber jacket sliced through the mist, his right arm swinging a rifle, his black boots trudging through the dewy grass. A long way behind him, curious sheep looked on, waiting for the fun to begin. A shot fired up into the air. I thought my ears would crack.

'Shit, shit.' The van phut-phutted a few yards. 'Let's run,' I said.

'How can I? Honey, help me.'

'Quicker,' I said. 'Quickly!'

There was another shot that clipped my wing mirror.

'Jesus, Duff, I can't do this.'

'Fuck,' I said. 'No time, no time.'

My chest burned. Our wheels slid in the mud. Nerys kept her cool and her foot down hard on the accelerator. Somehow, we managed to move away to safety. We turned a corner and approached a row of new-builds. I saw Fiat Pandas and manicured hedges, *normality*.

'That was a close one' I said.

My wife didn't answer. With a shaky hand, she steered us on.

There was a joy about being on the road with Nerys that pleased me, no, made me nigh-on delirious. I loved the smell of her hair, different but the same. I loved the curl of her toes on the pedal, the whiff of smoky sandalwood on her wrists. My wife was a firecracker, my dangerous weapon of choice. I got to thinking, had life always been this pleasurable with her around? Had life really been so much better? I answered in the affirmative and I asked myself why this should be.

They say there's someone for everyone – they *say*. But if you ask me, there aren't enough people to go round. I should know. Twenty years ago, I'd won Nerys over. Twelve years ago, she'd agreed to be my wife. In the ten years that had passed without her, nobody else had been able to fill the void. Oh, I tried all kinds of shapes and sizes: those who wanted me, those who didn't, short hair, long hair, dyed black, natural. But they'd been too small to fit the Nerys-shaped mould.

Cara. Cara was still raw with the hurting and hurt can turn you raw. Nerys hurt me. I tell you, raw's not a state you want to be in. Your skin turns to glass. Everyone can see your insides. I didn't want to be that man. I didn't want to be the man made of glass.

Another problem: Perhaps most thorny of all, there remained my girlfriend, the tight-fisted Angharad. For the time being she was still in the picture, for better, for worse. The neighbours all knew about her, with varying degrees of affection. It was Angharad who had told me those weasels at The Faculty had been plotting to get rid of me. Then, there could only be one man behind the betrayal: a bloated fool with a superman complex. I'd last been summoned to Saul's room three weeks ago. It had been a rainy afternoon.

'Duff? Are you still with me?' Saul tapped my hand with a wooden ruler. 'I was just saying your diet's working – or are we not paying you enough?'

I faced him at his fold-out table. As was customary when I was in his office, I leafed through his research notes. They were handwritten and I could barely make out the words. As a rule, at The Faculty, we took it easy. You might say we worked to rule. Anyway, Saul's notes looked much the same as they had the last time I flicked through. This time, though, there was a new name in the footnotes.

'Ah, thought you'd notice. You must have heard? No? Wow. Well, that's Rory Adler – only 23. Quite astonishing, quite something. An impressive orator. Yes, so good he'll be joining us. He'll be taking a junior post in the Autumn.'

'That's good,' I said as I looked down to his feet. His shoes were the smart, soft-leather kind. They had a block heel. I wondered how much he earned to afford shoes like that, but I knew I'd never find out. Saul was as guarded with his wage slip as he was about his private life. He'd had affairs, I knew that much, but I knew to keep quiet.

Alone in the van, I opened my eyes to see a shopping trolley glide past perilously close to the van. I shouted at the simpleton pushing it to be careful. Slyly, I watched Nerys approach. She climbed in and we soon found ourselves back in the land of hedges and gravel driveways. Nerys whistled and hummed.

'Cara's fine. Nothing major to report.'

'Good,' I said. 'Daryl still with her?'

'Daryl? Sure. They've been making Welsh cakes. Or so she says.'

I cracked my knuckles. Nerys tutted. She hated the sound, I knew that.

So, that afternoon, Saul looked at me hard and for a beat too long. He had something to tell me.

'Go on,' I said.

'You know Duff, there are easier ways to earn a living – a better living. Your local pub: do they need staff?'

I looked straight into his dishonest blue eyes.

'Well, the pay will be better,' I said, as calmly as I could in the circumstances. 'But my whole week spent in the pub? You don't expect me to go where the real action is, do you?'

Saul clicked his tongue as loudly and self-importantly as he could muster.

Nerys shook my shoulder.

'Duff? Are you with me? I was just wondering if you've taken your medicine? Only your snoring, it kept me awake half the night.'

With her spare hand, she cupped my knee. The road was smooth and quiet and there was green all around. Not a house in sight. Sweet ecstasy.

'You heard me through the van walls?'

I'd been convinced I'd lain awake most of the night. There'd been matters on my mind, festering, refusing to go away. Nerys had been back three days, but so far she'd shared little of her life back in Santa Fe. When I thought of her life over there, I pictured a nest of bees.

'What do you eat in America?' I asked.

'Eat?'

'Eggs and chips, tacos, fajitas. Those funny wrap things – what?'

My wife kept her eyes forward and her mouth neutral.

'All of those,' she said. 'And more besides.'

'And do you like teaching?' I asked.

Nearing a mini roundabout, she slowed, waiting for me to give directions. When none were forthcoming, she took the second exit and we coasted along a quiet, tree-lined road with identikit houses. She kept her grip tight on the wheel.

'I have to do it, but I'd rather not, so – '

'And the students?'

'Oh, they're okay. Hard not to resent them. They take up my time – time better spent. I sit there with my ideas and I picture what I want to do with the sewing machine when I get home.'

I wondered if she was lonely over there in Santa Fe. Apart from a string of failed lovers, of which I was the trophy-holder, her personal life was a lost cause. I sensed Nerys stiffen at my questions. I knew not to push.

'At least the roads are wide now,' I said with a forced brightness. 'I thought the bracken back there would poke its way in. Wrap its tendrils round my neck.'

'Well, I'm relieved too,' Nerys said. 'My head hurts from having to steer so hard.'

We floated downhill for a bit. Front gardens were stacked together, like they were huddled together for warmth. There were kids out pushing, prodding, punching. We passed a man weeding in a shirt and tie.

'We can take a break?' I suggested.

'No. No, not yet,' she said. 'Let's press on.'

Slowly, she loosened her grip around the wheel. Once again her knuckles were a pleasing pink. By my estimates, we were just under three hours from the coast. So, I sat back and peeled open a bar of chocolate. I offered Nerys a bite but what I wanted was to feed her one chunk at a time, like I used to. Greedily, she grabbed a square and took a delicate nibble. Nobody could nibble like Nerys. It was all in those sharp teeth of hers.

I was happy again, content to coast along on the tarmac. I looked around me, forwards and to my sides. In the wing mirror, I spied a white Citroen cruising close to our bumper. The bonnet was dented and the plate dated it somewhere back to the mid-nineties. Nerys sped up.

'Ah, Goddamn,' Nerys said.

'What's up?'

She looked down to her foot on the pedal.

'I have cramp.'

'Stop then,' I told her. 'There's a place just there – no, there, that's it.'

We edged up to the gate of a private property. It was the type of house mere mortals like me could only dream of owning. She climbed down and crunched over the gravel. I watched her press her foot down hard.

Swansea. We had married on a rainy, warm Tuesday. It had been a dark-brick church with low, wood beams. Nerys's mother had chosen the chapel, where she herself had married. There had been confetti, cucumber sandwiches, supermarket wine. There had been a single-tier wedding cake and cheap party favours. The Labour club.

When we'd finished our first dance together, Mack, my father, waded in. 'I'll show the wee thing how to move,' he said. From the side, I watched her hoof drunkenly around in her Meringue. Mack, whisky-fuelled and fired for romance, held her up. Everyone was there, except for the Medusa. 'One of her headaches, son.'

Nerys's family had been a carefree valleys' clan. Their only wish for Nerys was for her to experience marriage and children. Simple. But I wondered how much we knew of each other back then. I'd been blind to the significance of that day, buoyed as I was by enthusiasm. Nonetheless, I'd been stoic about our chances of a successful future together. Maybe we would last, maybe we wouldn't, but in the meantime I was committed to giving her all she wanted.

I wondered if Nerys had shared my vision for the two of us. I suspected she had been grateful to be spared a worse fate with a valleys boy. Perhaps I had exploited that fact. What I failed to consider was the possibility that Nerys would one day leave me. But I couldn't have painted over the cracks in her psyche, any more than she could have pretended to have been happy in our quiet house miles from anywhere, with only the animals for company.

All we are, all we can be, can be traced back to our childhoods. My home had been quiet, contemplative and messy. Nerys's had been noisy, intuitive and orderly. As adults, either we seek a similar pattern, or we seek a punchy alternative. I should have known then Nerys was seeking the thrill of the new. It worked for a while, until we discovered our respective shortcomings. So, it was inevitable Nerys had saddled her horse and moved on.

But moved on to what? To whom? A similar chaotic experience to be repeated ad-infinitum? The same old pattern of mistakes: a Scientologist, a businessman, a lesbian. Interesting for a while, a short fix of happiness, but we should have talked more. I should have lent her my books.

'That better?'

'I get cramp a lot,' she said. 'But darn it. I've lost my bearings. The map. Where should we go?'

'According to this, left at the next junction.'

I took a whack of my inhaler, breathed in the dizzying high and closed my eyes.

'Duff? 'The brook over there – look!'

'Hmm?'

'Pretty, isn't it?'

I opened my eyes.

'Ay well, I guess you'll be brook-starved over in Santa Fe.'

My wife's nostrils flared. Her look said: *Enough, Duff, your sniping: it's starting to grate.* So, to please her I cooed over the brook for a bit – coo, coo – but I couldn't shake what Angharad had said to me in my bedroom last week.

Saul had been slowly wrecking my career from behind the scenes. There was no doubt in my mind. And my illness was just the excuse he needed to dig the knife in deep. Slowly but surely, my slacking had been an affront to him, The Faculty, to all of them. Obviously, I had my reasons for shutting down, but the question remained: what *was* it I wanted? For sure, I'd fallen out of favour at The Faculty, but I'd fallen out of love with the job. My face didn't fit. There was nothing I could have done about that. Nerys nudged me.

'You okay hon? Too hot in here?'

'Do you remember Gene?' I asked. 'Gene Feldman.'

'The Doctor? God, yeah, course I do. Fancied him something cruel.'

'You did?'

'God. We all did.' I detected a hint of mischief in her grin. 'Why, hon? Don't tell me you're going to give me a thrill. Planning on inviting him along?'

I could take that. Nerys, like Angharad, enjoyed a little game.

Angharad. There had been times when I thought I knew

my girlfriend, but those times had been when she was under my watch – as for the rest of the time… I wondered. Would Cara tell her about Nerys and me? If she decided to, I feared the wrath of my girlfriend. Those sharp cheekbones of hers matched her sharp mind. I shivered. The thought of a vengeful Angharad caused a pain in my abdomen. A flying fist.

In this life you're all too often prodded, pushed, and slapped around. I'd thought Dr Gene Feldman would be a friend for life. We'd known each other for more than twenty years. What I had come to expect was some loyalty. Last month, he'd agreed to see me at his practice, but only to humiliate me.

I found myself in Harley Street. In a small room, facing a row of Turners, all swirling waves and bouncing foam – reproductions, I imagined – I waited. Experimentally, I opened a copy of Tatler and threw it back down on the glass table. Gene came to fetch me in pointed brogues. His chest heaved behind a crisp, white shirt. He smiled at me in the same way he's always done.

'Good of you to stoop to our level, Duff. I mean, I didn't exactly expect you to show up. I assumed this was some kind of joke – a hoax, perhaps?'

He nodded me over and quickly ushered me to his room. I ran my hand across the length of his desk.

'Solid oak?'

'So then, where to start? Assuming you're here with your tail between your legs – what can I do for you?'

'I'm unravelling, Gene.'

I was direct. This was a private practice, against everything I stood for. I didn't want to hang around a second longer than I had to.

'Shoot,' he said.

So, I told him about my breathlessness, my lacklustre lectures, Cara. Ever since Nerys had left, I'd been worried about her, her sorrow, her tantrums, her dead-eyed smile. Gene leaned forward and pulled the lid from his expensive pen. He rolled it to and fro across the desk.

'So, it's a shrink you're after, old man? Happy to recommend one. Mind, it'll cost you.'

Gene slammed his silver pen down on the desk and foisted his chair back. I looked past him to a portrait on the wall, a green and bloody face in turmoil. I coughed and swallowed down a wave of acid reflux. I coughed again.

'Well, I have to say you look shagged, Duff.'

'Thanks?'

'But as you're here, let's take a look at you. Let's look at that naval you've been gazing at all these years.'

Nerys tugged at my elbow.

'Duff?'

'Hmm?'

'You with me? I was just sayin' – why did you mention Gene just now?'

I sighed and rubbed my face.

'What? What's up?'

'So, you really fancied Gene?'

'Of course, I told you.'

Gene's room had been sterile and smug, the kind of place that lacked a heartbeat. The metal had been cold against my chest. I had fought hard to keep my eyes open.

'Deeper man, from deep in your belly! That's it. Keep still, man. Better. Righto, I'll send you down for a scan.'

'What? Now?'

'Now.'

My wife slammed on the brakes. A shadow swept across the bonnet. A heron flew low.

'Let's watch it for a while,' she said. 'I've missed this. The wildlife: it's different in Santa Fe.'

I took a long ram of my inhaler. Wheeeee. I glanced at the green fields either side of us.

'Do you remember that time in Barry?' I asked.

'What? When Cara was a bab? How could I forget? She was unbearable that day.'

'You were upset that night,' I said.

'When?'

'After that day out in Barry.'

Nerys started up the van.

'Was I? But I thought she'd love it. Building sandcastles. Feeling the foam on her feet.'

'I told you we'd laugh about it one day.'

'So you say, hon, but we didn't, did we?'

I remembered. The sea had been a pale moss-green. Cara had sobbed uncontrollably. She always hated the sand beneath her feet, chafing those tiny toes of hers. We'd gazed at the chalets stretching over the horizon. They were dismal, concrete breezeblocks, crumbled and neglected. Auschwitz-by-Sea, I'd quipped. Nerys had wanted to cry along with her.

It had been a humiliation needing Gene's help. After my scan in the basement, I'd been disorientated and bruised. In a haze, I headed back to his room. I opened what I thought was his office door, but cardboard bowler hats – vomit bowls? – crashed down onto my head. Gene found me slumped with my face in my hands.

'Well, you've certainly given me a giggle, old man. I'm really glad you stopped by.'

Gene escorted me out. The sun shone bright. Timidly, I held my hand above my eyes, like a makeshift visor. He squinted back at me.

'Two days, Duffy. Can you wait?'

But my old friend Gene had no intention of calling through with my results. In fact, he didn't even return my calls. That was the last I heard from him.

Like a great, puffing lion, I took more rams on my inhaler. Nerys looked at me with a curiosity that bordered on pity. So my wife had fancied Gene. Well then, I'd show her. Ahead of us, soaked-through in a diaphanous T-shirt, my Big Chance waited under a sign to Dunbar. Her small thumb hovered above the curb.

'Stop,' I said.

'No, no, you must be kidding. Duff, no.'

'That's mean,' I said. 'She'll catch her death. We've got to be good Samaritans. It's the right thing to do. Look!'

'What?'

'Look. There. She's gawping at the magic bus. She'll be expecting us to stop the van!'

'No!'

The rain pelted hard, flooding the bonnet. I grabbed the wheel. The girl jumped back, fear transforming her face. Through the streaming rain, I made out her face, pretty and heart-shaped. Her bra hung low. There was an inch of mottled breast.

'Jesus, Duff, what d'you think you're playing at? You might have killed the poor girl.'

'And you were happy to just pass on by,' I said. 'I guess we're both bastards.'

'Honey, that's not fair.'

With trepidation, the girl tottered in her heels over to my side of the van. Her lank hair blew. Her white legs were as thin as my inhaler, with two round saucers for knees. For maximum effect, for sheer theatrical fun, I looked her up and down. A man half-starved was the look I was going for. Pretty much the truth. Nerys nudged me.

'Well, aren't you going to open it, then?'

I groaned at the thought of surrendering my personal space. My clapped-out lungs needed room to breathe.

'Um, hello Miss?' I said, cautiously. The girl looked at me with a hard-edged smile.

'Dundee?'

'Pardon?'

'How far up yis going? That's where I'm heading to.'

My wife sighed. *Great*, she said silently.

'Aberdeen,' I said cheerfully. 'Hop on in. We'll take you as far as we can.'

The girl clambered in. The leather squeaked. Above us, the black sky cleared to a translucent grey. The rough road ahead stretched to the horizon.

'Not a soul around,' I said.

I admired her high heels, cerise and tarty, impractically high. I'd never been a heels man, but now I was prepared to make an exception. The girl had makeup caked on too. Her skin was creamy. I held out my hand. Limply, she shook it.

'The name's Duff,' I said. 'And this here is Nerys. How can we help you, Miss?'

'Alrigh'?'

'And what's your name, Miss?'

Nerys took a deep breath. On the exhale she made a simpering sound.

'Kirsty,' she said.

'Oh ay, what's your mission?'

'Eh? My mission?'

'What's taking you to Scotland today?'

'Oh, right yeah, got an interview.'

Kirsty flung her rucksack down by my feet. I pulled my knees up higher.

'A job?' my wife asked.

'Nah, college. First time for me.'

I kept my grin wide and bright.

'So, what's the course?' I asked.

'I paint – acrylics, waters – dabble in all kinds of stuff.'

Perfect. Nerys would be forced to try and bond with her now.

'Oh, yes?' Nerys asked, with a flatness that delighted me.

'Faces mainly. Fluked a distinction in my Foundation. Scared I'll muck up the interview though. Can't do the talky stuff. Scares the crap out of me.'

Kirsty pulled a pot of lip balm from her bag and smeared it on thick. More perfection.

'What do youse do, then?' Kirsty asked, neglecting to look at either of us.

Nerys opened her mouth to speak but closed it again.

'Nerys is a fashion designer, a successful one. I'm a lecturer.'

I listened to myself, allowing my job title to hang proudly in the air.

'Oh ay? What kind?'

'It's complicated. In layman's terms a bit of Sociology, a bit of Psychology. A side order of New Media.'

'Ken?'

'Yeah, told you it was complicated.'

So, with my spiel over with, I listened to them chat together for a while. As I closed my eyes, I recalled fragments of last night's dream. It had been a sweaty, semi-wakeful affair, visceral and strange. A wind blew up from deep in the valley. There were coconuts, lazy waves, happy-sounding street names – where? The Domincan Republic – no, Jamaica? Yes, or St Lucia. My body was serene. I flexed my chest expander. Then, as the wind whistled up, I flew inside a wind socket. Walls narrowed and darkened. There was a brilliant white light.

'Duff? Kirsty's asking you if you'd move over a bit.'

I shunted over and took a moment to enjoy another look at Kirsty. She obviously worked out. Her leg muscles were toned, like rope. It would be easy to pretend I fancied her. But Dundee? I sighed. Sometimes I could be such an idiot.

'My boyfriend, Robbo. Another reason I'm getting away. He tried to stop me. Said I wouldn't fit in with the clever set. Said they'd all be odd but I'm even weirder.'

'Nice of him to say,' Nerys said.

'Ach, he's probably right, but it gets me away from him.'

My wife scrunched up her nose. I could not deny there was a strange odour. I suspected it might be fish and chips. We watched Kirsty rummage in her bag. She pulled out a bundle wrapped in tissue.

'Want a nibble?' she asked me.

Nerys kept her eyes on the road ahead. The steam rose from her pasty. I wondered where she could have bought it from. We hadn't seen a shop for miles.

'There's a garage. Just back there behind the trees,' she said, reading my mind. 'So d'you wanna bite or not?'

Shyly, I nibbled a corner but my wife refused to look. Trickles of rain fell against the windscreen. Nerys switched on the wipers and I gazed out. The cows were tranquilised by the harsh weather. The fields looked an odd colour, like the earth was bleached by the rain. Kirsty smiled, gummy and sincere. I edged closer until we were shoulder to shoulder.

'How would *you* do it then, Duff?' Kirsty asked.

'Pardon?' I said.

'How did *she* do it, exactly?'

Kirsty pointed to the book at my wife's feet. My wife liked dismal, confessional poetry, quite at odds with her latest taste in music.

'Who?' Nerys asked.

'Sylvia Plath.'

'Why?' I asked.

Kirsty brushed the crumbs from her lap and wiped her mouth.

'What if... ach, forget it, yeah?'

Kirsty felt around in her bag and pulled out an aerosol. She sprayed under her arms. The smell of tangerine was a sweet relief.

'Because, yeah, what if you mess up. And all you end up with is brain damage? Then you'd be a vegetable. You'd need help to finish the job. Someone to take you out.'

Hearing this, Nerys cleared her throat. The temperature dipped suddenly. Kirsty crossed and uncrossed her legs. I wondered if she could use a blanket.

'I thought about jumping,' Kirsty said, 'but I hate heights.'

'Could be exhilarating,' I said.

My wife's lips curled downwards, and I wanted to laugh. Both women treated me to a quizzical look. I tapped my wife's thigh, but she yanked her leg away. Good, I thought, this plan of mine was working. I listened to the air, ambient in the rain. My door rattled in the wind.

'This all sounds a bit desperate,' I said. 'Can't be as bad as all that, surely?'

'Sorry to hear that, Kirsty,' Nerys said in a school-teacher tone. 'But it'll be exciting at college. New faces, new adventures. I loved my time in art school.'

'I dunno, though, it's a bit y'know, selfish – ken? My parents – they're fucked. Dad had a hotel, went bust – bankrupt. They think it's a waste of time.'

We passed a dreary-looking strip. There was a chemist with the shutters down; a bookies; a graffiti-strewn newsagents. People lived here, around and about, but they didn't have to. I wondered what was wrong with them. Nerys pulled over.

'Now, why don't you show us some of that stuff you have in your bag?' Nerys suggested.

I wondered what she was getting at. By the look of Kirsty's face, she did too.

'Your paintings,' she said. 'You must have them on you if you're off for an interview.'

Kirsty held up small sheets of oil paper, around ten in all. The images were dry-brushed and blurred. Not the type of thing I liked at all. So, unable to offer any thoughts of my own, I took a moment to conjure The Bubble, my treasured, transparent haven, my coping mechanism. I closed my eyes and pictured rainbow colours caused by droplets of my own breath. The light circled around until the bubble burst.

'Duff? I was just saying these are very promising. Nice use of light. I'd say Kirsty's a budding Richter. A possible Tuymans – maybe.'

'Oh ay?'

But I didn't hear the rest of what she had to say. I had a sharp pain in my chest. So, to calm down, I took two long rams on my inhaler. I blinked. Our wheels flew on smooth tarmac past quiet cottages and bright postboxes. My stomach burned. I kept quiet.

'I have tunes,' Kirsty said. 'Interested?'

I pointed to the tape player. Smokily, Kirsty laughed.

'A cig, then?'

She thrust a packet into my chest. I yelped as she flared up a fierce-flamed Clipper. The smell was herby, familiar, lucky cow, but there was no way I could join her, not with Nerys at the wheel. I knew not to push.

'Ooh, do you mind? It's been a while,' my wife said.

'Here, suck it down. I have more,' Kirsty said.

And I looked at Nerys smiling for the first time since Durham. Well, well, well. Driving and indulging in a little marijuana, my wife, the renegade.

Kirsty lit another. She handed it to me, but before I could settle it on my lips, Nerys stretched her arm across and wrenched it from me. She gave it back to Kirsty.

'Not in his condition,' she said.

'So, when's he due?' Kirsty said.

'Don't mind him. He's had pneumonia. He's showing off. Don't encourage him.'

I looked up to the sky. A fine mist had replaced the rain.

Neither drifting left nor right, the clouds appeared to quiver. My feet itched. I took off my trainers and pulled my socks off. I threw them in the back.

Silently, we rolled on to a small town, indeterminate and damp. People came and went, some dived in shops, others kept walking. Beside me, Kirsty giggled, so I looked down to see the source of her amusement. A dry wisp of Old Holborn was peeping through the zip of my trousers. I was not only a human wreck, I was an embarrassment too.

I couldn't shake the feeling something vital was missing from my plan, and I had a hunch what it could be. My game was missing a wee dram of *joie de vivre*. My heart wasn't in this Kirsty charade, not nearly enough. It had been a stupid, knee-jerk reaction inviting her along.

From the pavement, I watched them talking and laughing behind the grime-spattered glass. My treasured magic bus looked handsome in the sun. I admired the thick rubber of the wheels. To the casual eye, it looked worn and rusty but the windscreen shone, smears and all; it was mine and mine alone.

Our wedding day in Swansea had been a joyous affair. I had been proud to save my wife from her family's low expectations. I was unable to give Nerys the riches she deserved, but what I could offer her was a haven where she could be herself.

When her mother was alive, she had fawned over my

academic status. She had touched my collar, imagining the cotton to be of the best kind. She had mistaken my second-hand shoes for Bond Street finery. I'd been too busy enjoying her attention to correct her.

I wandered in to the chemists. The pharmacist, all silver hair and yellowing teeth, slammed her pen down on her paperwork. She peeled her glasses from her nose. I watched them dangle from a string, like a hypnotist's pendant. Patiently, I hummed. I checked my watch. Five past four. I was hungry.

Nerys's family had been a Bible-loving bunch, fanatical about the Old Testament and, like most church-goers, the scriptures had been everything to them. Nerys cherished her own copy of the Children's Bible. I remembered the blue hardback, Samson and his haunted, blue eyes. Ay, they were wonderful fairy stories, I told her, if you like that sort of thing. She told me she used to love Sunday school. No doubt it was an escape for her.

So, with my trusty sucker-pills in my back pocket, I stepped outside to see what the girls were up to. I scanned the quiet scene. A fat dude in a Thin Lizzy T-shirt passed in front of me. The way some men grew goatees; they were *anti* women. I turned left. There was a woman hiding behind expensive sunglasses, a brown mac buttoned up to her neck. A guy brushed my shoulder. I wondered where the hell he needed to get to in a hurry around here.

Then, in among the cars, I spied a white Citroen. I glanced around the car park for the driver. I scanned the shops. There was a supermarket, a hardware store, countless other places.

Strange, but there was no mistaking the bonnet was the same, like someone had tried to hammer out the shape of Mexico in the steel.

My wife returned my look. It was then I saw she had her arms around Kirsty, sobbing under her blonde, lank fringe. I wandered over, yanked open the door and slammed our lunch down on the dashboard.

'Two cold bacon rolls. A little present for you both. I've eaten mine. Sorry. Couldn't wait.'

'Wow hon! You love bacon? What a fascinating character you are.'

'Sorry. I completely forgot.'

Kirsty devoured hers. I wolfed the spare, it was only small. My wife made do with a pre-wrapped samosa from her rucksack. I felt guilty – but not too guilty. Kirsty had stopped crying at least, so I shunted an inch closer. Brazenly, I draped my arm across the back of the seat. My wife sped off with her knuckles white.

The cars whizzed past, furious and blurred; they made my eyelids flicker. I leaned forward and switched the radio on, thinking of all the songs I'd wrenched my insides out to over the years. I glanced at Nerys, straight-faced and biting down on her lip. The year we met, Ace of Bass had been in the charts, Nirvana too. 1993 had been a terrible year for music.

Kirsty smiled at me – ay! A flirty smile, for sure. I sat up and edged my arm further around the back of the seat. I tapped Nerys's shoulder to make her aware of what I was doing.

'Duff? Is everything okay? Because if you like, you can drive for a bit? You're probably itching to.'

'No, I'm fine,' I said. 'You carry on. You're doing a fine job.'

Kirsty spritzed her hair with some more of that sweet-smelling aerosol. I sighed my relief.

'Has something died in here?' Kirsty asked. 'No offence, like.'

'Have you changed your T-shirt lately?' Nerys asked, looking at me.

I grinned. Naughty, but deserved.

We parked in a field, approximately forty miles north of Berwick. My eyes fixed on the barbed-wire fence. There were no farm animals here, just endless grass and a high wind. Nerys and Kirsty announced they were off to shop for beer and I enjoyed a moment to myself. Since Nerys had been gone, I'd made a point of trying to fill my life with all manner of chinook, trying to turn my empty life into some kind of a story.

Before Angharad had arrived on the scene, I'd had another woman, Ruby, much younger. She'd been different from my usual type, demarcated by the fact she had a shaved head. We'd met in Bloomsbury at a *Women in Film* conference. The following day we'd had our first date: a wind-swept Sunday.

Ruby sat in the graveyard, her feet barely touching the floor – swinging, swinging. Her purple pumps shone under a Kensal Rise street light. She couldn't have been more than twenty. Reclining on the bench next to her, I watched her pour coffee into a polystyrene cup. Later in the day she invited me back to her flat. There, I'd let her run her hands all over me. She had certainly been a strange one.

'What's the matter, Duff? Are my toys putting you off? Just shove him over there. That's right, just there. He's Humpy the Elephant. Mad really, should have moved him – all of them out the way.'

Ruby lay under me. Her blue lamp faced away from us, shining a dull moon on the wall. Her bedclothes had been fusty and the damp, peeling walls hadn't helped my libido. So, to compensate, I imagined her as Nerys – Nerys with her hair long and her eyes determined and hungry. But it had been no use.

'What's the matter? If you like – now, if you're really good – no, I know – I know.'

I wondered what she was getting at.

'I can show you the things I can do with my toys.'

Now, the shock must have shown in my open mouth because Ruby grabbed my jeans from the floor and threw them back at me. I swiped to catch my jeans and missed. With my travel pass still valid for another hour, I rode the bus back to my hotel. After that, I missed Nerys more than ever.

I decided I was only human. My grief was such my impulse was to escape. People do need to escape from time to time. The farm had long depressed me. What bothered me the most was the torture of having to watch the animals and Cara go without. Myself, I cared little for. Cara had been losing weight. She had plans of her own. She had wanted to study

English Literature in London, but I couldn't support her. We were limited by our circumstances. The stakes were high for the both of us.

My wife handed me a mug. The enamel handle was so cold I pulled my sweater down over my hand. Kirsty sat close to the fire, toking on a spliff. I wondered how many she had in that bag of hers. We resumed our chat. Stories of the terrible places we'd visited.

'Woah, that place was a *total* dive,' Kirsty said.

'Oh ay?'

'My only time abroad. Krakow. Thick fog. Jewish Quarter. Jesus, the place was haunted for sure. There was a voice in that attic room. I swear it. It boomed in my ear. Get out! It said. Get out!'

'In English?' Nerys asked.

'Yeah,' she said.

The sea swirled in the distance. Closer, the smell of salt reminded me how little fresh food I'd eaten lately. I pictured plump, ripe shellfish. The brackish taste would go down well with a cool glass of Muscadet or two.

My own attempts to make wine as a money-saving venture had been a disaster. I'd tried elderberry first. Through pity, Jones the Warren had offered me bags full of berries, but my finished product had tasted less like wine, more like undiluted Ribena. It had plunged me into new depths of misery and want.

Nerys cracked open a can. I studied her. Through the swirling gloom, she appeared to be smiling.

'The worst place I stayed might have been in Aberdeen,' Nerys said. Typical Nerys, she could never follow the game.

'That doesn't count,' I said. 'We agreed it has to be somewhere we stayed on holiday.'

'Oh, dope must have gone to my head. Alright then, France. When I was a kid we stayed on this campsite by the sea. Blistering heat rash for two weeks. It rained for ten days – and one of our coach party...' She stopped and laughed hard, '...was shot – actually shot – in the toilets!'

'Where was that?' I asked. I was sure she'd never mentioned this before.

'Ah, near Biarritz somewhere. I forget now.'

'Fucking Poland,' Kirsty said.

I couldn't deny Kirsty was a feisty one.

'Duff, your turn,' Nerys said.

'It was like...' I stopped; it was painful to remember. 'Like a self-catering thing. It was pretty much – you know the type of thing.'

'Where?' Nerys asked.

With the smoke rising, I struggled to make out my wife's features. She must have heard this before and I didn't want to bore her. I hurried through.

'Fishguard,' I said. 'We turned up, and it was like the windows were broken. There was mould everywhere. It was basically like no-one had been in it for a year. There was no heating – freezing – ay. In the garden there was an Old English sheepdog. Only three legs. Mack – my Dad – booked us into a B&B as an emergency measure. I'm pretty sure the holiday only lasted a few days.'

I waited for them to stop giggling.

'Desperate,' Nerys said.

'Fucking mad as fuck,' Kirsty said.

'Yeah, laugh away,' I said, 'but what's the bravest thing you've ever done? I could get by in a tree if I wanted to.'

'What are you talking about?' Nerys said, rubbing her face in concentration.

'I got mugged once,' Kirsty said. 'In Aberdeen. Shot him straight in the eye with my Pepper Spray. Risky, but – his legs, man. He ran off down the street. His limbs all fucked. Ran straight into a shop door. Fell in a heap. Sweet, it was.'

'That was brave of you,' Nerys said. 'Was it in broad daylight?'

'Nah, the early hours. He was a customer. One of the sleazy ones.'

Through the smoke I saw my wife swallow. Sometimes Nerys could be so naïve.

'Go on then, Duff, your turn, let's have it,' Kirsty said.

'Bow,' I said. 'There was an incident. London. A pub. A dark place. Drunks falling about everywhere. On the tables. Out the back. Filth. There was a City boy in a fleck suit. Remember them? Essex probably. Started bragging about all the money he earned. Kept calling me a northern twat. Tosser. I was doing my first job, just a temp, office thing. Minimum wage, a summer job. He was a total slick-haired Loadsamoney type. But he wouldn't let up. He kept on and on. My hair was long – well, I say long, it was below my ears at the time. But I didn't look as fey as him. Wanker.

'Dark times back then,' my wife said. 'So?'

'I told him a woman came up to me earlier, sniffing around, asking for a blonde guy in a suit. Had I seen him? I told him she was gorgeous, waiting outside. Well, no bloke can resist that, can they? So he went out and I followed. Then, when I caught up with him, I pushed him against the wall. Smashed my pint glass on the floor. Held a shard up to his neck. His eyes nearly split out of his head. All twitching muscles. I was a thug, but God, it was sweet. I spoke to him in a low voice – so low – I thought then – that's it, that's all it needs. No blades or guns or anything, just a low voice.'

'God, what happened?' Nerys asked.

I looked for signs of my wife swooning. There was a glimmer.

'He legged it,' I said. 'The spineless cunt. Anyway, job done, that took care of that.' I smiled. 'Now then,' I said, grinning at my wife. 'It's your turn.'

'Me? Do you really need to ask?'

'I do,' I said. And I did need to.

Kirsty was crossed-legged and swaying now. She was giggling, but at what, I'd stopped trying to guess.

'Wait! I've got one,' Kirsty said. 'Falkirk. The summer.'

I fought down a groan. 'What time's your thing tomorrow, by the way?' I asked her.

She laughed and my wife laughed along with her. I sensed the penny was about to drop.

'I was trying it on, like,' Kirsty said.

'It's not til next week,' my wife said and giggled into her hand.

Right then, I decided as soon as it was morning, we'd shake Kirsty off and leave her in this field, friendless and without a bean if we had to. Nobody was going to get one over on me. Let alone that tiresome skank.

In bed alone, with my nose pressed to the ceiling, I heard them giggling away in the tent. I closed my eyes and remembered another dream I'd had recently.

In sheets of hail, sweet, serious Ruby pulled up at the gate of the farm. Cara ran out to her Mini, her heels clicking down the path. From the driving seat, Ruby turned her head and stared back at me watching her from the window. Her eyes were globes of black ice. The car flew up under the belly of a heavy cloud.

I'd thought about setting up a small, online business, but I couldn't decide on one. Moreover, I had no idea where I could find the money. Sinclair had suggested I made T-shirts with funny captions, but I knew the net was awash with similar ideas. The truth was I didn't know where to begin and it seemed easier to stare at the ceiling and hope for the best.

The following morning, I woke to the smell of fuel. A hand shook my arm.

'Duff? You okay?'

Slowly, I opened one eye and raised my head. I could see the fleshy part between my wife's neck and breasts. Her skin was dappled by time's claw.

'Alright?'

If I moved my head higher, I risked headbutting the ceiling.

'She's taken it all,' Nerys said.

'Taken what? How?'

Nerys didn't answer. From my rictus position, I heard her open the door and head out. I rolled over and slid down. I pulled on my jeans.

Outside, she frowned. To emphasise her point she upturned her purse. A tiny photo of Cara fluttered onto the grass. I picked her up. A mere bairn.

'Have you checked yours?' she asked.

'Checked my wallet?'

'Yeah, stupid.'

I didn't understand how Kirsty could have been in the van without me noticing, but sure enough, the wallet I pulled from my pocket was empty. My wife sat on the grass and handed me her brush.

'Do it for me.'

'How?' I asked.

'Just like that. No, not like that, faster. Much faster.'

I brushed so hard I was afraid I'd hurt her.

'What's wrong with you, Duff? You're not assertive enough. Harder!'

But I didn't want to. I threw the brush down. In a playful mood now, I grabbed her head and locked it in my arms. She laughed.

'Shall we?' she asked.

I shrugged, unsure whether or not I could trust her, but I

followed her inside her tent and watched as she peeled off her clothes. She lay down waiting for me to leap on top and, with a wide grin on my face, I took what was mine.

Nerys could be a mysterious woman. She was turned on by the strangest of circumstances.

Still, you can never say for sure. Benevolence can bite you on the bum, and meanness can come up smelling of roses.

On this trip, I had learned a great deal about my wife. She could be compassionate in the face of competition, Kirsty was proof of that. As for me, I could be self-interested and calculating, willing to help only when there was a tangible benefit to myself. I wasn't proud of this, but still there it was.

So, in the early evening, after we'd cancelled our cards in a local bank, we carried on up the coast, drawing closer to the purple heather and the blustering wilderness.

'Wait! There! Did you see it?'

'What, hon?'

'There! Did you see it?'

She puffed out her lips. Damn full lips.

'?'

'The windscreen,' I said, 'it seemed to quiver!'

She looked at me, but inanimate objects, I was sure they had a soul.

'It seems things – I don't know, like they can breathe.'

'What, are you crazy? It's just the vibrations.'

But I knew different. Occasionally, back at the farm when Cara was out, I'd sensed things move. The first time I'd noticed this was the night after Nerys had left us. I'd slammed my palms flat on the walls to steady myself. The ceiling had heaved itself up and down above me. While my insides wracked with the pain of missing her, the ceiling had moved with me in my sorrow.

'I could use a drink,' Nerys said.

'Should we not find a spot to set up camp first? That would help,' I said. 'Then I can relax.'

'No,' she said. 'That's the boring option. I want to hang loose for a bit.'

'Fine.'

So we found a quiet bar by the sea and parked up. The fierce waves blew foam against the sea wall. The breeze was thick with the stagnant smell of seaweed. I could have gagged.

We headed up the steps to a hotel and went inside. It was one of those seaside bars, all white, wooden panels and miniature plastic boats. Nerys opened a purse that was once again full. We discussed whether or not to report Kirsty to the authorities.

'She's probably making a career out of it,' I said.

Nerys pinched my arm. I pinched her back.

'Show a little concern for the poor girl, will you? There wasn't much damage, was there? I only had a fistful of dollars on me. I can live without it – it's not as if she had a choice.'

'Seriously?'

'Yep, it's hard for her, you must admit.'

'But she's a criminal,' I protested.

Nerys tutted. She crossed her legs and leaned forward across the small, round table.

'Honestly, Duff, the bank – you heard what they said. We cancelled the cards before she had the chance to do some damage.'

But now I was distracted. On the other side of the room, a man in a candy-striped suit was staring over. He was all bulging flab and popping buttons. He looked kind of familiar although, with a face like that, I felt sure if I'd met him before I would have remembered.

'Look at him,' Nerys said. 'I'm surprised that wicker chair can take him. You can hear it creaking from here.'

'That'll be my lungs you can hear,' I quipped.

'Good God, oh no, he's actually coming over.'

With his trousers tight around his candy-coloured crotch, he rose from his seat and walked towards us.

'May I?' he asked.

'Ay, go on,' I said.

I nodded to the vacant chair that would have to suffer the weight of him. Slowly, he eased himself down and from his pocket he pulled some mints. He offered us one. We declined.

'A holiday, is it?' His voice was all mucus and adenoids.

'Maybe,' Nerys said. 'We're on a voyage, visiting my parents in Aberdeen. See, my dad's on his last legs. It's all been so sudden. You know how it is. Finally mum persuades him to go to the docs. The first time in his life, then whack! This happens. Typical men though, I say. So, I'm sorry we were just, y'know talking… privately. We're a bit upset, you know?'

Clever, I thought. But this didn't seem to faze the guy.

'Never can resist a pretty face,' he said. 'But if you're looking for a real man, why don't you shed him and come off with me?' The man laughed, Nerys didn't. 'Joking, joking. Just ignore me, can't resist.'

He sat back, oh-so-pleased with himself. Nerys managed a smile.

'So, if you don't mind?' Nerys hinted again.

'Ah, yeah, but I couldn't help noticing your campervan out there. You don't see many of 'em these days. Taking you all the way, is it?'

He peered outside to the magic bus resting by the stone wall, magnificently splattered with spray.

'So, like I was saying,' Nerys said again, but louder this time. Tinny chart music started up in the background. Fatso tapped his knees, leaned in close to my face and grinned.

'The *Women in Film* conference,' he said. 'That's where we met last. You're Duff Boyd, aren't you?'

I rewound for a moment. Good God, it couldn't be.

'Not Dan Winterson?'

'Yep,' he said. 'You went off with Ruby, remember?'

Nervously, I swallowed down the rest of my orange juice. Nerys moved first. With perfect grace, she held out her hand.

'Nerys,' she said to him. 'Technically, Duff's wife.'

He kissed her hand and looked deep into her hazel eyes. He was like a – Christ, he was nothing but a boozy lothario.

'*Technically* enchanted, I'm sure.'

Nerys smiled and I was surprised to see warmth behind it.

'By rights I should take you outside, Duff. But by the state of you, it wouldn't be a fair fight.'

There was no doubt, Winterson was a revolting slug, sweaty and hoggish. His eyes were like pig nuts, as good as *buried* in that slothful face of his. Still, I had to admire his front, bundling over here with no sense of danger. I looked at him and wondered how it was possible to put on so much weight in so short a time. *Dirty old man running his hands all over me,* Ruby had said. No wonder she'd come running to me. Winterson squeezed my arm. I looked down. He released his grip.

'Only kiddin'. You were welcome to her, Duffy. That cow was fucken bonkers.'

And I remembered what Ruby had told me about Winterson. He'd been impossible to shake off, she'd said. His beard smelt of stale butter. His armpits had reeked of sour grapefruit. Enough, I'd warned her. But I had doubtless been the excuse Ruby had needed. Anything to escape Winterson.

'So, what's your dad's fate, then?' Winterson asked Nerys.

'Pancreatic. Ripped through his body like a – well, at a rate of knots.'

A tear fell from my wife's eye and bounced off the table. An amazing display to behold.

'So, your Lovemobile…' Winterson said. 'Do you think it'll get you there? Got a cosy little gang-bang going on in there, have you?'

I looked out. It was still there, my beautiful baby. Nerys looked at me.

'So, who's your friend?' he asked us both.

'There's just us two,' I said.

He leaned back and his chair shrieked a warning. 'Yeah, right. So, what's new with you, anyway, Duff? You still teachin'?'

'Yes, just a bit of part-time lecturing, you know. Same as ever. You?'

'Nah,' he said. 'The kids, they gave me a grilling. Couldn't control 'em, so moved back up north. In showbiz now. Play the trombone.'

This at least was interesting, but Nerys looked less interested. Slowly, she sipped her drink.

'A jazz band. We've had a few gigs. A few down in London. Money's shit, but it beats teachin',' he said. Winterson smiled. 'So you're not planning a gang-bang out in that thing, then?'

'No such luck,' I said.

Nerys kicked me under the table.

'So who was that I saw, then? The dude in the hat? Who was that?'

'You saw a bloke by the van?' I looked out nervously, but the van was alone in the car park.

'I dunno,' he said. 'Might have been. Might have been a woman. Hard to tell these days. Couldn't see much. So it's just the two of you, then?'

'Yes,' my wife said. 'And if you don't mind, we've got to go now.'

'Right,' he said. 'Don't let me keep you. But look, if you

fancy a drink back in your field, or wherever you're parked up, I can follow you?'

Our look told him that would be a hateful idea and we mumbled our goodbyes. From the van, we watched him supping alone at the window. Nerys blew her lips hard and I kissed them but the good feeling wasn't to last.

Ten minutes later on the quiet road, a mint Peugeot loomed large in my wing mirror. Hard, pig-nut eyes peered at me from behind the wheel.

On an unlit road, Nerys swerved under a huge horse chestnut. The wheels slid into the damp mud, disturbing my gear in the back. I heard my belongings scatter themselves across the floor. We waited and held each other's hands. United, we watched Winterson's car shoot past.

'Too close,' I said.

Shaking with fear, not least because her own manic driving had almost finished us off, Nerys flicked the lights back on. Our eyes adjusted. We wondered what to do next. Across the road was a large, wooden hut. Plastered on the orange door was a clipart drawing of a man with wild hair and brown teeth. A bubble caption advertised a night of comedy.

'Fancy it?' Nerys asked.

'Sure,' I said.

I didn't care much what we did, as long as we were alone. I'd never been a fan of forced laughter, but we paid our money and took our chances. We took our place at the end of a row of school-assembly chairs.

My view was restricted by a line of lads in front. I twisted my neck to peer past them – great, just wonderful. I glanced around me. A granny knitted a baby shawl. A bored flat cap sat with a sausage dog at his heel.

The act was terrible. An old-timer in a toupee raced through a riff on women drivers. It was a weak, woman-hating attack, a retrograde spectacle if ever I witnessed one, but Nerys honked in my ear like a woman fresh out of jail.

When we left, it was black and cold. I was glad. Black was what we needed to bed down for the night. So, we found a field and set up camp in a wide, limitless space, quartered by low hedges. I started up a fire. Nerys grinned. Waving a rolled magazine, like a conductor's stick, she fanned the flames. Flecks of paper dotted my clothes, like tiny fire flies. I brushed them away. She handed me a lager.

But the truth was, unlike Nerys, I had felt sorry for Winterson. There must have been a good reason for all that weight gain, all that thinly-veiled passive aggression. I wondered what his story was.

'Don't you think it's odd?' I asked Nerys. 'Winterson around here?'

'No doubt about it,' she said.

I put my arms around her, but she wriggled her body away. She cracked open another can.

'What is it you want from this?' I asked Nerys, with a candour that surprised me.

'Meaning?'

'You know what I mean,' I said.

Nerys looked down at her tanned legs and gave a long

sigh. I waited. She unfurled the magazine and fanned her face. On the cover, David Cameron was sat with a patient. The patient was a hand, no more, gripping the side of the bed.

'I was curious,' she said.

'?'

'Life is complicated back home.' She smiled at me. 'Some things I regret.'

Rubbing her face, she closed her eyes to absorb the heat. I wanted to touch her.

'Here, give it to me,' I said.

With a pen pulled from my pocket, I doodled a moustache above Cameron's bloated lips.

'Nice,' she said. 'But hang on. Wait here a minute.'

I watched her disappear inside the van. Headlines, headlines. I shot through the pages at lightning speed. The Romanians were coming, apparently. I willed them to come and to bring some of their gorgeous women with them. What else? There had been two pence added to the price of beer. Big deal. Farmers complained of yet more taxes. And on, and on. I threw the mag down. I thought about Cara, her pony, the cockerels, Daryl. Nerys returned with her cardigan tied around her waist.

'Have you heard from her today?' I asked.

'No, I haven't. And now you mention it, will I call her?'

'Why don't you text her?' I said. 'But text her much later.'

Nerys sat down next to me. Breathless again, I took a ram on my inhaler.

'Aren't you worried about her?' Nerys asked.

'Maybe,' I said.

A bird chirped, loud and clear. I blinked away dust from my eyes. The smoky fire wracked my chest to bursting point. Lazily, I sniffed my T-shirt. It smelt of charred wood. Cold again, I buttoned up my blazer.

'So...' I said to Nerys.

'So?'

We heard a crunching sound. A shadow loomed over David Cameron's face. Slowly, we twisted our heads around. Under dark eyelids, Winterson's eyes seared us. Nerys gripped my leg.

'Any more cans stored away in the Lovemobile?' he asked. 'Because I thought I'd lost you there for a sec.'

Time stuttered, rooting us to the ground sheet, until I couldn't be sure it was my own hand gripping my can or a plastic one.

'Sure,' Nerys said. 'There's one or two. Would you like one?'

She sounded shaky. Winterson didn't answer. My wife went to the van to fetch him one.

'Thought you were giving me the brush-off for a moment there, Duff.'

'No, not a bit of it.'

'Cos I was sat there in the bar thinking to myself, what the hell is he doing up here? Seemed too much of a coincidence. A long way to travel for an apology, isn't it? You needn't have.'

He eased himself down. Too fat to cross those mighty thighs of his, he reclined back on his elbows. His trouser buttons bulged under the strain. The candy-stripes were dulled by the gloom, but no less audacious.

'Fortunes come, and fortunes go, eh Duff?'

'Oh, ay,' I said shivering and I glanced around for my blanket, but there was no sign. 'Eh? Come again?'

'Now, don't look so worried. Why don't you tell me more about your little lady back there.'

He nodded in the direction of the van. I hoped Nerys was planning to return.

'How did you get together, then?' he asked.

'Um, well we married a while back, in 2000. June 2000.'

'So, you're an adulterer too then?'

Ah, Ruby again. Let it go, man, you'll develop an ulcer.

'No, I don't think so,' I said. 'Thing is, it's complicated.'

Nerys returned and handed him a can. She sat close to me. Together, we watched him glug it down. Slowly, he crushed the can in his hand.

'I've been doing a bit of research – a bit of this and that,' Winterson said. 'Easily done these days – Internet and that. Still talk to Saul now and again.'

I coughed, which was difficult enough in the circumstances with the smoke poisoning my lungs. I moved an inch to the right. Nerys shifted too. She draped her hand on my lap.

'But enough about him,' Winterson said, and I breathed out my relief. My chest sounded close to breaking. 'No, see, it's Ruby I want to talk about.'

I stole a glance at Nerys. Patiently, she waited. The fire burned low. I gave it a shove with Cameron's head.

'Here, help with this, will you?' I asked Winterson. 'Poke it there, that's it. Flares up good that way. Not too much. Ay. Done this before?'

'Not been up this way for a while,' he said. 'Fun though, innit? Plenty of wood. Nice and private. No-one around. No-one comes near here. Roads are rough and slow down this way. All black. Black as your hat. Mind if I have this?' Winterson pulled another can from the plastic. 'Sometimes, yeah, sometimes shoot up this way when I fancy burning the midnight oil.'

'Oh ay?'

Nerys put her cardigan on. She rocked gently back and forth.

'I like birds, see,' he said. 'Don't know much about them, mind. Like the smell of the ground up here. Back to nature and that.' Winterson looked at me and grinned. 'Stars out here.' He dropped his smile. 'Ruby, just such a – all the fucken shit. After me getting a crap – fucken shit gig, no money.'

Nerys gripped my knee again.

'You're still sweet on Ruby?' I asked

'Why d'you wanna know? What's it to you?'

'I just wondered.'

'She's fucken nuts – just looped out at me – did a proper mental. Right there.' Winterson thumped his chest. 'Just pulled it. Right there. Because the pain, you know. Really hard, the force, you know? Spat daggers. Right there, hard as nails. From nowhere. Just came at me. Pulled a knife. Had to get my balance. The force.'

'God,' I said.

'Jesus wept,' Nerys said. 'What happened?'

'After all the – cleaned me out, she did – my cash ran out – cleaned me out – keeping on, keeping on. What could I do? All the shit – all the bar jobs – teachin', couldn't get a gig. Christ. Right here – all the – never felt anything like it.' Winterson rubbed his chest better. 'Caved in though, didn't I? Just another tenner, yeah right! Blown right back in the chair – all the shite – one more ask, I thought. Then, bam! She asked – a twenty – just til Frid – '

'Wow,' I said.

'No,' he said.

'No?'

'No. That's when – right there – she pulled it – a blade – in the kitchen – the table – no-one around, no witnesses.'

He whipped up his billowing white shirt. Sure enough there was a pink circle buried deep in mounds of flab. I groaned. Poor Winterson. Nerys got up.

'Sorry you guys, don't mean to be – but I'm wiped out,' she said. 'I'll have to leave you to it.'

Helplessly, I watched her crawl into her tent. She zipped it up to the top and tugged once more for good measure. I wished I could escape as easily.

'Just stabs me right in the chest, no, there. Touch it.'

I got up and did as I was told. What else could I have done? 'Jeez,' I said. My index finger brushed the hard edges. He grabbed my hand and pushed my finger inside. I could have thrown up right there on his shoes.

'She just pushes it into me, right in there. I just sat there. Her face was – like she couldn't believe she done it. The knife

– she dropped it – clang, right there on the floor. Then, the cow ran.'

'Ran where?'

'The door – open, it was – bang, behind her. Gone. Just like that. Last time I saw the bitch. This is the baby.' From his pocket, he pulled what looked like a butter knife. 'Yeah, look – stubby blade, brown, curled handle, couldn't slice cheese – not even butter. Couldn't slice through shit, but it sliced through me. Yep, this is the bugger, the same one. Touch it.'

I did. It felt blunt.

'Didn't the police need that?' I asked.

'What for? What the hell?'

'Evidence?'

He snorted, piggish and loud.

'Told you – all the fucken shit – all the times I bailed her out – and this. But I didn't report her. She – God no, she was my *girlfriend*.'

The fire died completely. A wind howled past my ears. Nerys's tent buffered behind us and Winterson hauled himself up. With his eyes narrow and mean, he gripped the knife, blocking my path. I zig-zagged past him but he mirrored my movements, making my tongue burn in terror. I ran to the van. When I was safely inside, I slammed the bolt across. I waited, frozen in time. I imagined him stood there hating me – hating me more than he knew he had the power to hate. Then, as coolly as you like, I heard him crunch away.

In the morning, I tried to make sense of me and Nerys, Nerys and me. My wife had been back a week but so far she'd remained tight-lipped about life in Santa Fe. I only had the bare bones of a story and here she was giving me another chance – why?

'Duff, you okay?' I lifted my head a centimetre or two.

'Eh? I think so, why?'

'I heard something – a rustle – a car rev. Is he still here?'

Nerys leant against the door with her arms crossed. Her knees shook.

'Don't be daft,' I said. 'He went – last night. I'm sure of it – definitely.'

I lowered my head and listened to the van door slam. From the slab, I heard the clang of tent pegs, the sound of unzipping. I did the turtle shift and watched her through the window pack away in the mist.

With my head clear again, I slid down from my bed and scrambled around for my notebook. I lay flat on my stomach to have a thorough look. Then, with my lungs heavy, I searched the front, the dashboard, the glove compartment. I waved my hand around under the seats. When I went to find Nerys, I found her face down on the grass in a dog pose.

'Have you seen it?' I asked.

'Seen what?'

'Don't mess, Nerys. My notebook. My bloody receipts.'

'Of course I haven't,' she said, panting. 'Where did you leave them?'

I scanned her dismantled tent, a flattened mink. There was no sign of the notebook. Nerys stood up straight.

'I heard strange noises this morning – rustling,' she said. 'I – thought it was you but you were…right there – behind the van. Duff, listen to me, I'm telling you, there was someone here.'

I rewound to last night and pictured Winterson's fierce eyes, the blunt blade, the dash to the van with my mouth blazing. But even before all this, there was no way Winterson could have broken in and stolen my notebook. The van had been locked – what's more, he'd been with me the whole time. I would have noticed if he'd vanished, even for a second.

'Well, if you don't have it, then we have to go look for it,' I said.

Nerys bit her lip. She shifted on the grass but my mind was firmly made up. My most private thoughts were out there somewhere in unsafe hands. I imagined kids tearing strips, mimicking my voice – och ay, I love you sweetheart, you're my life, my soul, my *everything*. I pictured them laughing, kicking the pages around a beach, setting fire to them. I couldn't bear it.

'The bar. We'll go there,' I said. 'That has to be the obvious place.'

We settled back in the van and drove off. Rain trickled down the salt dust on the windscreen, creating tiny inlets. The morning was foggy and the miserable Hammer House scene matched my dark heart. This was possibly the worst thing to happen to me – and on a trip where I planned to flex my dormant writing talent too.

'I don't remember taking it to the bar last night,' I said.

'What if Winterson's back there again?' Nerys said, steering us down a dirt track.

'It's the cold, light of day, what can he do?' I reasoned. 'Anyway, a crowded bar – that's probably the safest place to bump into him.'

We passed a cute stone cottage, Hansel and Gretel-like. A white poodle crouched on the grass by the gate. I saw Nerys's knuckles whiten again.

'Look, Duff, why don't you just buy another? See, there's a post office there. You can get yourself a shiny, new one.'

I shook my head. Sometimes Nerys understood nothing. Her phone bleeped from inside the glove compartment. I pulled the flap down but she snatched the phone from me. Feverishly, I took a whack on my inhaler. I breathed out long and slow.

'You're driving,' I said. 'Only trying to help. Avert an incident.'

'Yes, *but,*' she said.

'Who is it, then?'

My wife scanned her eyes down a text message and grunted.

'Cara. A letter from her college – yada yada – trouble.'

'What? What's up with her?'

Nerys slammed the brakes so hard my forehead buffed the windscreen. I tell you, I could have done without it. Cara's crisis could wait. I had one of my own. So, I left Nerys and dashed in to the bar to speak to the owner. I peered out through the large sash window and watched my wife hold her phone to her ear. The owner came back. Nothing doing, he told me. I pleaded with him to check with his colleague, a boyish voice I could hear in the kitchen. Surely, someone had seen it. No, he said.

Dizzy again and with my throat rasping, I returned to the van and grabbed the passenger door handle to steady myself. I clambered back in.

'So, where else could it be?' I asked my wife. She didn't answer me. There was a beat.

'Aren't you going to – ?'

'?'

'Cara,' she said.

Nerys got out and perched herself precariously on the beach wall. There was a steep drop to the sand and I willed her to be careful. From the comfort of the van, I heard the muffled croaks of arrangements being made. My chest tightened. I took another long ram on my inhaler. My notebook was most likely being kicked around somewhere. The thought made my head tighten, fit to burst.

So I made use of my time. I checked the bins in the car park, retraced my steps back up to the hotel door. I rummaged in the bushes that neatly lined the steps – nothing. I floundered around in the back of the van, scanning the same nooks and crannies I had already checked. When Nerys had finished on the phone, I settled back in my seat and blew my lips hard.

'So?'

'Now listen, Duff. Don't get cross with me. There was an incident. She's had a letter. She kept it from you, she said. Not her fault, she said. I told her – Daryl – I could hear his whiny voice in the background. Anyway – '

'Christ, what is it?'

'Now look, don't. She's on her way up.'

'Hasn't she got college work to do?' I said, aware how desperate I sounded. 'Doesn't having the house to yourself mean anything these days?'

'Don't panic,' she said, 'it's not serious.'

'How can – ?'

'I told her we'd pick her up from the station. In a few hours.'

'Which one?' I asked.

'Berwick.'

Nerys fondled the wheel and started the engine.

'But this will ruin everything.'

So, with my lungs clapped out, and my energy as depleted as the van's fuel, we drove on to the nearest garage.

We found ourselves at Berwick station an hour before dusk. My sore mood would not abate. After a long nap in the van, I was woozy and listless. By contrast, Nerys was vivified after a trip to town. Her new hooped earrings shone in the fierce afternoon light.

'Duff?'

'Yes,' I said. 'That's my name. Well done.'

My wife thought for a moment.

'Who is Andy?'

I had no idea. Andy?

'Only Cara mentioned an Andy came to the farm, asking after you.'

So she *had* come. Just as I thought she would. I shook my head.

'No, that's not – that'll be Angharad.'

'Yes, that's it. Who did I say, then? No, Angharad, you're quite right.'

I watched my wife pull out her phone from her jeans pocket and step down onto the pavement. She made a call. To Cara's mobile, I imagined.

I thought of the day I had first met Angharad. It had been a warm day in late September. Angharad had been introduced to us in The Faculty as the new department administrator. With our heads down and our brains struggling to focus, the staff meeting began. The speakers droned on. I sensed their eyes on me. Angharad had been minute-taking, doodling – what?

Angharad could not reasonably be described as a great beauty. Some might say she was plain, but I had immediately identified her as my type – insofar as I had a type. I had always been impressed by women who refused to try hard, who were aware of their natural, God-given power. For the most part, I liked women who attracted men to them like flies to pure honey. My desire had not burned for Angharad. I had not ached for her or willed her to fill the space between my sleepless body and the peeling wall. But Angharad had stubbornly failed to notice me. Perhaps this had been the attraction.

'So, who is she?' Nerys asked.

'My girlfriend,' I said, as flatly as I could.

'Oh, I see.'

Nerys looked down to her nails, twisting her wrists, like a cartoon secretary.

'*Was* my girlfriend. To be fair, it's been dead in the water for some time now.'

I decided with Nerys, honesty was the best policy.

'Hmm,' she said.

'Nerys?'

'The seven thirty,' she said. 'The train. If it's on time, I should go to her now. Stay here, I'll go look.'

'Wait. About –'

But she slid the door shut. She clicked over to the platform in those tan, leather heels of hers. They shaped her ankles nicely, making her legs seem longer – clever. I tried to push my irritation down. My own wife had denied me a chance to explain. So, I decided what we needed was a nice meal. With the wine flowing, she would be forced to listen to me.

The car park was quiet. I admired the simple station. A large, rusty clock hung between two arched windows. As I waited, I sensed a familiar writing itch and I twisted around to retrieve my notebook, but of course, it wasn't there. Instead, I settled for an idle gaze out of the back window. It was then I saw it: the same car with the same crushed bonnet.

So, I slid over from the passenger side and fired up the engine. I edged away from the curb, figuring I had at least ten minutes to play with before Nerys came back with Cara. Even allowing for my cloudy, drugged-addled brain this had to be pursued. I was certain this was more than mere coincidence.

I slipped along the road until I met with the busy, rush-hour traffic. Shops became blurred, white lines. Through manic eyes, I tried to make out the figure driving, but all I saw was a hat – a wide-brimmed hat. Anxiously, I put my foot down, but there was no way I could keep up. The shops faded to nothing and they were replaced by signs for the motorway. On the motorway, the engine spluttered and I was forced to pull into the hard shoulder. Defeated, I watched the Citroen vanish into the eye of a low sun.

Wheezing heavily now, I flipped open the glove compartment. I scrambled around for Nerys's phone. In auto-pilot, I pushed aside a pair of gloves, a bag of half-eaten sweets, a scarlet lipstick, but she had her phone with her. Of course she had. So, weaker than I'd been since the trip started, I found myself far from the station with no means of letting my wife know where I was. I deliberated on what to do.

When hope was at its lowest, I watched a mint Peugeot pull up behind me. A grinning Winterson stepped out.

Winterson rapped on my window. I took a few shallow breaths and tried to calm the confusion racing in my brain. I barked at him through the glass and asked him to tell me what he wanted.

'Just open the damn door, then.'

There was no game-plan for this. I stayed where I was, my arms stiff by my side.

'Are you following me?' I shouted.

'What – me? Open the passenger door, will ya? Will you

just open the damn door? That's it, just lean over. It's bloody windy out here.'

Winterson cut across my view. He looked small and stooped out there with the traffic whooshing past his ears. Sluggishly, I leaned over and opened the passenger door. A puffing Winterson bundled in. He looked pale. He smelt bad, of stale booze and cheap Lynx.

'Do you have something of mine?' I asked.

'Eh?'

'After you left, I looked around, pulled my bag apart, ripped the van sideways. No sign.'

Winterson's cheeks turned pink. I wondered if he was still angry with me.

'What are you on about?'

'I had a blue book, just a small one,' I told him. 'But it contained some sensitive information. I'm sort of keen to get it back.'

I decided softly, softly was the best approach with Winterson.

'Like a notebook?' he asked.

'Yes,' I said. 'Exactly like a bloody notebook.'

'Nah, not me,' he said. 'What's all this about anyway? Do you think that's the sort of thing I'd do, take something that belonged to you?' His look, well… it was *hard*. 'So, why don't you ask your friend, anyway?'

'Who? Nerys?'

'So, you're in a pickle? Tell me, then, what the hell are you doing out here, anyways? Where's the missus?'

Winterson's cheeks faded to a blotchy puce. He grabbed

the neck of my T-shirt and read the caption across the front. The word FOR was faded, splashed with bleach. He laughed.

'Bombs are for bullies, eh? You're fucken nuts, Duff.'

His breath smelt of warm bacon. He gripped me tighter until I could hardly breathe.

'Please,' I said. 'I've been in hospital.'

'Eh? What you sayin'? I'm barely touching you.'

His laugh, Christ, it was a real boomer. He pulled me closer until I was eye-to-eye with the crusty stain in his armpit.

'I'm delicate,' I said. 'Nearly died. I shouldn't even be out here. Nerys – '

'Ah, lovely Nerys.'

He let me go. I could breathe again.

'I just wanted to say hi, you know.'

He looked hurt I'd given him this cold welcome. Trust me, you don't want to see Winterson's hurt face.

'You wouldn't even open the door. Not nice that, is it Duffy?'

I managed a smile.

'Sorry, yeah, I know you only wanted to help. Thing is – '

'So, how can I?' he asked.

'Eh?'

'How can I be of assistance?'

Oh God, please God. Yes.

'Can you drive me back? Only, I'm not up to – I'm breathless.'

I sounded faint, like a coin dropping down a well. I thought of Nerys back at the station. She would be upset by now – no! Fuming. To settle matters, I'd wanted to tell her how little Angharad meant to me. There was much we still needed to say to each other, plans that had to be made. Cara had better have an iron-clad reason for joining us.

'What do you want?' I asked Winterson again. 'How come – look – how come you found me out here?'

'I'm tailing you, Duffy, not following you, there's a difference.'

There was? Winterson tugged at his blazer. Huffily, he took it off and threw it onto my lap. I shoved his rotten jacket down by my feet. I didn't care. His sweaty weight next to me was too much for my gasping lungs and I struggled to think straight. Winterson twisted his body to face me.

'S'fucken cheap. Hate the north. Didn't want to come back here, did I?'

'I like it,' I gasped. 'It's charm – ow – has a charm of its own.'

Winterson belched. A wave of nausea rose in my throat.

'So, are you going to help me or not?' I whimpered. 'That bulge in your pocket – what's in there? A phone?'

'You got a tab?' he asked.

'A what?'

'A tab – a rollie.'

He grabbed my jacket from the floor and shook it.

'Don't smoke,' I said.

'Smells smoky enough in here.'

'Smoke lingers,' I gasped.

Winterson stared ahead with a mad but vacant look in his eyes.

'Always rainin' here. Always fucken poundin' it. Hate it here. I remember thinking it were funny.'

'?'

'Different rules down in That London, I thought. That's the sort of thing they do down south. Play around with other people's women. I bet the Royals all do it. Everyone in That London think their shit don't stink.'

'I'm not from London,' I gasped. 'I'm more like you than you think. Name your price. *Please.*'

Winterson's eyes fixed upwards – to what, I had no idea. He hugged himself for a moment and then he started to sob, a real splurge from the gut. It was a startling sound, like a cat puking.

'I don't want your money,' he spluttered. 'I want something else. Information. Ruby, you hear from her?'

I didn't know what to say. Winterson's eyes seared me as if I had something to hide. I had no idea how to comfort him. Reluctantly, I patted his back but the awful greeting kept coming.

'Year two. Together two years. That's when she started acting up. Stealing. Small things at first. A lipstick from Boots. Something like that – or eye shadow. Then, bigger, better. She had to go one bigger. S'fucken, I couldn't afford her. Just a tenner till Saturday. Never tried to get a better job to pay me back. Then, she just quit. No job at all.'

Finally, he stopped. There was just the sound of passing traffic.

'Forget her,' I said. 'Move on, will you? She's – ow – she was crazy.'

'Was funny,' he said. 'Me thinking you were stupid. What does she see in him, I thought. Does she like long hair? That must be it. I used to like you. Thought you were a good-un – everyone said it. But you got lazy, stopped making the effort. All the students said it. Yeah, thought you were stupid. And she kept on and on.'

'Who?'

But this was all leading nowhere. My breath heaved. I had to get back to Nerys. Summoning a wave a strength, I turned the key and started up the engine.

'No, wait a sec, I'll take you,' he said.

'*Now* please.'

'Duff this, Duff that. Duffing fucken Duff. S'fucken cheek, after I took her back and all.'

Defeated, I turned off the engine.

'She blamed you, you know, treating her like that,' he said. 'Sent her proper mental. She's out to get you – or she would have been. Had I not – '

I watched him blow his nose, slowly, deliberately.

'She wound me up,' he said. 'Had to get her back. Tit for tat. One more ask for a tenner – just one and bang! Took her up the woods. Fired one in the air. Didn't want to hurt her – just scare her. Ran like a chicken, she did. There was the runway, a plane real low. Ever noticed the planes round here, Duff? Lower than most. But I misfired, took out a pheasant. Or summat. Fuck knows. She ran, anyway. Off, she went. Like I say, tit for tat.'

He spread his legs and farted; it was a real squelcher. I

wound the window down. Lazily, he pulled a phone from his pocket.

'Here,' he said. 'What do you want it for?'

'Take this down, will you?'

I gasped Nerys's number. My voice was little more than a squeal forcing itself from my punctured lungs. I knew Nerys's number by heart. Winterson hammered the digits into his phone. The road ahead turned black and I passed out.

My hands couldn't clench them couldn't feel the cotton against my skin I should have been able to feel a brush of fibre or the weight of my clapped-out frame slumped down on the bed something surely but nothing just that pine bleach stench again pine bleach and warm protein a bitter voice howled out could it have been mine no it came from somewhere in the middle distance I faced the window and looked out to a courtyard that resembled a barren concrete yawn some view hazily I floated around in my morphine brain I was in a half-world half man half Duff Boyd with great effort I blinked and smacked my dry lips together I could hear talking laughter footsteps there was a woman her face inches from mine I could smell her perfume it was a heavy mixture of oranges with spices too *strong* darlin' I swallowed she was tall Asian important-looking I saw the biro in her pocket a speck halfway down at the seam of her pocket her stethoscope dangled the tubing converged glinting in the light she spoke in a soft whisper to the nurse something something morphine something something change the dose something something we'll need to watch him closely then the click of her heels faded to nothing I thought of my father Mack Mack was my father *was* my father I looked like him he'd been a great teacher unlike me I hated teaching those ungrateful students Tim my brother was my brother is my brother died before I was born the grief was there in Mack's belly it formed a tough thorax he wrote so many stories he wrote a story a day halfway across London Bridge I peered down to the rushing water in my head there was a strange dissonance a mixture of fear and free will a solitary tug boat bobbed on the Thames below I thought I could do it actually hold my breath and plunge right in I'd put one foot in front of the other and kept on moving Nerys had been waiting for me at the other side her coat buttoned up to her neck her arms open wide.

Nerys and Cara arrived. Cara stared down at her empty coffee cup. Her hair was cut short. She looked pretty in her Doc Martins and a dotted dress. I shifted under the sheets. With a strained smile, a nurse took my pulse. Sadly, Nerys looked at me. There was a sandy texture on my eyelids, she told me, dots of powder around my mouth. I looked old, she told me. My skin was blue. I looked older, much older.

Nerys pulled the sheet up around my chin and patted it down. Groaning with the strain of movement, I twisted left then right, but the sheets were itchy. I knew I'd develop a rash if I was left to fester much longer. Cara held my hand and rubbed her fingers over my knuckles. I'd forgotten what she felt like.

'The ward's nothing like on the tele,' Cara said. 'Where's all the action? Nobody throwing up. No-one shooting their mouth off in reception.'

Cara leaned over my face. Her nostrils were two narrow teardrops.

'So, will you join us up to Aberdeen?' I managed to ask.

'God, no,' she said.

She smelt of fresh daffodils. I wondered how. Was it March? No, that had been months ago. It was July.

'You're nuts, Dad. The doctor – he took us to one side – said it was cold at night. Couldn't believe you were sleeping in the van in your condition. Reckon he thinks you're mad – no heating, no rest – not the type of rest you need, anyway. We've got to get you home, Dad.'

Their visit was a mesh of me protesting and them insisting. When I was released from my bed and safely back in the van, I told them we must head on up the country.

'Dad?'

We passed an almighty jamboree of scraggy hay and tent tops. There was an Aunt Sally and rows of pyramid flags. I had to admire the pomp and ceremony of country living. Approaching the sign for Newcastle, Nerys indicated left.

'What's this?'

'What's the matt – '

'North,' I growled. 'The plan. We've got to head up. We've got to get to Aberdeen.'

'Enough honey,' she said as patiently as she could muster but I heard the strain in her voice. 'You're not thinking straight.'

'Up,' I said with more force this time. 'And what about the music? I told you we needed a soundtrack.'

'What?'

'Our soundtrack. REM. You said – what have you been doing? Did you download any?'

'Honestly, Duff, do you think I've had a spare minute?'

Dizzy again, I tried to grab the wheel but Cara blocked me with her arm.

'Enough,' my wife barked.

Under my breath, I cursed our daughter for being up here with us, scuppering the whole plan.

'Why is she – nobody's even told me why she's here.'

Nerys stroked her support down Cara's hair.

'Thing is, yeah, thing is Dad, it's like this.'

'She's been suspended, hon,' Nerys said.

'From college? Why?'

'Smoking dope,' Nerys said. 'Daryl – '

Daryl. I should have known. His name could just as well be etched on my daughter's face. The tell-tale pimple was right there on her forehead, for all to see. I slid my hands in my pockets. Well, that was it, I decided as soon as I was home, I'd tell Daryl he wasn't to see Cara again. Not ever. I regretted not having my phone with me, it was oddly disempowering.

'I'm hungry,' Cara said.

When we saw a roadside restaurant, I shouted to Nerys to slow down. If we were heading back down south my wife would at least have to buy us lunch, and I planned to have the most expensive item on the menu.

The place we arrived at was all orange, plastic chairs and

dark, empty booths. With a heavy heart, I pushed my watery potatoes around my plate. I tried to eat one but it was a fluffy cloud on my tongue.

'Shoot!' I said to Cara.

'Dad?'

'How long have you been smoking that stuff, then?'

Nerys frowned at us both.

'Since, like, forever,' she said.

But I didn't believe her, not that I would have minded if she had. With my history, I'd be a hypocrite to mind a little fun. No, my beef was with Daryl. I conjured his lank, brown hair and his skinny, hairless chest. He didn't care about anything other than fucking my daughter. That was reason enough to hate him.

'He's not to come again, for at least a month. Got that?'

'Eh? That's not – '

'Got that?'

'Mmm.'

'Right. Good. Decided.'

We watched our daughter finish off her burger and fries, barely pausing to grunt. Children are adaptable. Nerys had left her and the anger still burned, you could see the signs in her body language, stiff and guarded, but here she was ready to trust Nerys again. I don't think Nerys understood the damage she caused us. She couldn't have. No warm-blooded woman would have intentionally hurt us so badly. Yet she had left us. I watched Cara wipe her mouth with a napkin and I saw a glimmer of forgiveness flash in those sweet cheeks of hers. Young women have an open heart. It made me worry for her, but love her all the more.

Outside again, under a sky of white and grey, I stood back from the van and watched them clamber back in. The weather was turning cold. I thought about airing my clothes later in the evening, when we were all camped-up. I needed more layers, a bit of extra padding. Cara bounced down hard on the leather. She picked up a blue book from the front seat and flicked through. I pretty much shot over.

'What the – where did you find that?'

'Dad?' It was here, on my seat. I thought – '

I yanked it from her. Nerys looked at me.

'It was really there when you got in, bold as brass – right here on the leather – couldn't miss it?' I asked. Cara shrugged. 'And it definitely wasn't there when we left for the restaurant? Think, dove, please, it's important.'

'Dad, I think I would have noticed if I'd been sat on shiny paper. Look, my legs are bare. It would have clung to my flesh. I would have had to peel it off. Look, right? I would know, yeah?'

But to me it made no sense, made no sense at all.

The wind blew but the dust on the roadside refused to stir. By rights, I should have had my sails battered and my spirit knocked flat by another hospital stay, but I was oddly ebullient.

I didn't want to head south. South was no place for Duff

Boyd, and I decided if I could only banish Cara, I could work on Nerys.

At the wheel, Nerys looked drawn and tired. More than anything, I wanted to be with her in her tent, re-railing our plans, and asking her about her life in Santa Fe. Besides, with my health at an all-time low, she could hardly expect me to sleep in the van.

'Daryl will be missing you,' I said.

With her cheek pressing against the window, Cara looked at me. She acted as if this illness I had was contagious.

'Whu? But you said – '

'I know what I said. But it was little more than a knee-jerk reaction. You're forgetting I remember what it's like to be young. He'll be pining for you. Cruel to keep him waiting around with only the cockerels for company – no?'

'But he's – '

'Nope, he'll be lonely,' I said, 'and I've been thinking: the chooks. No sense in him doing all that work alone. Don't want to make him cross.'

So this was convincing – yes? I could picture my mouth moving and the words tumbling out. It was a warm display of empathy that could fool even my clever daughter.

We pulled into a garage. Nerys stepped down and slammed the door shut. Together, we watched her waft the attendant away and fill the tank herself. I took the opportunity. I grabbed Cara's arm.

'Angharad, has she been round again? Only I was thinking – '

'She said she's going away for a few days. Munich – with

a friend. She was just making sure you'll be back soon. Now, let go of me?'

Cara tried to pull her arm away but I kept my grip tight. Cara didn't know the extent of my debts, how much Angharad had been hounding me to return her money. Angharad had lent me enough to pay for animal feed and had supplied me with enough cash for me and Cara to see us until the end of the month. The caveat was she was the boss. She would have power over me for as long as I needed her help. I'd lied and said I'd have the money in a week or so. Foolish. Trouble followed me around.

'She's been just the once?'

'Yeah, she came on Sunday. The day after you left. Now let go of me!'

I released my grip and flopped my hands on my lap.

'She hasn't been again?'

Cara crossed and uncrossed her ample legs. She had her mother's thighs.

'I told you, she's on holiday, for another few days. She's busy, Dad.'

'Did she ask you where I was? Did you tell her?'

She sat up and fixed her eyes on her mother inside the garage paying up.

'No, I didn't tell her, but I wouldn't be too cocky if I – '

'What?'

Cara smirked. 'It's like I wouldn't bet on her not finding out.' I wasn't sure what she was getting at. 'Come on, Dad. The neighbours will have seen you ride through the village in this thing. It's like the curtains, yeah? They twitch, yeah?'

At Berwick station, we stood facing on the pavement by the blue door. We looked up to the handsome clock and the tall arches. I pulled out some of Nerys's cash from my wallet and thrust it into her hand.

'Ta,' she said. 'So, how's it going, then?'

'Eh?'

'You know,' she said, rubbing her hands.

'Oh ay, fountains of fun,' I said. And I knew she would catch my meaning.

'Not so well, then?' she asked.

'She won't talk to me,' I said, 'not properly, but now we're alone again I can probe her. Sound like a plan to you?'

'S'pose. When will you be back?'

'Not sure,' I said. 'A few days or so?'

Cara turned her back on me and walked to the blue door. I hated that she had such low expectations of her mother. When there is nobody there for you, it can turn you hard. But back in the van, I soon forgot about Cara and I was high once more. There was all to play for. We headed off. The signs for Durham flashed by my smiling face until it dawned on me we were heading south.

'What's this? No, let's carry on up north,' I said.

Nerys pulled over and switched off the engine. She turned to me.

'So, this is all about you now?' she said. 'I don't have a say? Don't forget, Duff, it takes two to tango. If we carry on who knows what'll happen to you. Goddamn it, I'm beginning to think you're crazy.'

She stared ahead at passing cars and pouted. I turned to her and stroked the inside of her knee. She used to love that.

'Well…on one condition,' she said.

My clammy stroke slowed and I took my time to pleasure her warm thighs.

'Name it,' I said.

'Lindisfarne,' she said.

'?'

'The Holy Island.'

'I know what it is,' I said. 'But it's south of here. We're too far up! It's south of – '

'We go there before Aberdeen, or we go home,' she said. 'You know damn well I've always wanted to go there.'

She smiled at me, a lovely half-circle. So, with the map resting on my lap, we set off again. I was willing to concede.

Perhaps, I considered, I was enough for my wife. Finally, she was in need of someone who understood her, and here I was about to wave the little, white flag. It was true: my looks were fading; my crow's feet were darkening; my hair was peppered with white – but I loved her.

That bastard Gene.

'Remember that time Gene threw a party?'

'Who?'

'Gene,' I said.

'Which party? There were a few?'

It was true: he was a popular bastard.

'The Seventies one,' I said. 'I wore flares and that polyester shirt – remember?'

Nerys slowed down as she remembered.

'I hated those sweat stains in your armpits – gross.'

'Ay, no amount of washing would remove them.'

We'd snuck away from the party and dived on Gene's bed. The evening light was low. Through net curtains, the late sun struggled to reach us. Nerys wore a purple roll-neck and beige platforms. I'd run my index finger along the length of her palm.

'You'll have a long life. I told you that, remember?'

'Hmm.'

'Remember, upstairs?'

'Oh yeah. I remember now. You were nothing but a dirty gypsy. A phony.'

Slowly, we coasted in the left lane. I grabbed hold of her left palm. She let me.

'Ah, one day you'll have a son,' I said. 'There'll be a bouncing boy with red hair.'

'And my love line?'

'Ah, well see, there's a break just under your middle finger. But don't worry, the break ends there. Then, it's darker, stronger than ever.'

Nerys pulled her hand back.

'Hang on,' I said.

'I don't need help in that department, thank you,' she said with some bitterness.

Lindisfarne was a gritty kind of pretty. We watched the high, wooden resting posts, like bird huts. Calmly, the green sea stretched ahead. The air smelt alive and we breathed in the smutty mud flaps and the crusty salt dunes. We made our way over to the hotel.

The place was all swirling wallpaper and dark, polished oak. After Nerys had checked us in, we took to our room. The manager, a blue-eyed wonder-boy rapped three times on our door. Nerys opened it. Reclining on the bed, I eyed him suspiciously. He wore beige chinos and a linen jacket. He was preppy looking with a smarmy smile. Nerys gushed – thank you, thank you, three bags full, really, couldn't want for better.

At dinner my wife looked pleasing. There was a slick of gold glitter across her eyelids. She wore a cotton, paisley dress. I loved natural fibres and this delighted me. My wife was once again the Nerys I understood.

We sat at a mahogany table in the centre of an empty room. Meditatively, we listened to the rain. Steam coated the windows. The salty wind wafted in, cooling us. Finally, I had a chance to sample some fresh seafood. Nerys ordered for us both. She sounded hungry.

'Nice, but I thought – '

'Nope, not now. Don't look at me like that,' she said. 'If I see another mushroom on the menu, I'll holler.'

'But Cara had been so impressed you were vegetarian now.'

My wife shrugged. I took a sip of warm water. There was a coldness in her look that made me swallow.

'Look, Nerys, about Angharad, I – '

'No need,' she said. 'That's your business.'

'I thought you'd understand,' I said. 'Angharad – it's over, really.'

She polished her knife with a napkin and looked around her. I changed the subject.

'Tell me, then, what happened with Winterson? How did he do it, exactly?'

'?'

In the soft candlelight, my wife's hazel eyes looked beautiful

I thought back to my last meeting with Winterson. Before passing out on the hard shoulder, the last thing I remembered was giving him Nerys's number. He'd punched it into his phone with those great, bloated hams of his.

'So, he called you?'

'Of course he did, of course he called me. He was the last person I wanted to hear from, what with Cara up and all. All that business. God Duff, what do you think you were playing at?'

She circled the inside of her elbow with her finger. She always did this to comfort herself, I'd noticed.

'So, he drove me to the hospital? And he called you again when I was in? He did all these kind things?'

'Yup,' she said.

Well, well, well. I flicked the rim of my glass and enjoyed the sound of quality crystal. The smell of tarragon wafted in from the kitchen. A piano started up in the next room. An easy-listening tune I couldn't place.

'Do you remember the time you tried to teach her the clarinet?' I said.

'Clarinet? When? Ah, yeah, she couldn't do it, could she? No matter how much I – '

'Painful, wasn't it?

You tried to warm her up by asking her to blow in tissue paper, remember?'

'No, no, not like that, like this. God, she wouldn't be told, would she? I wrapped her little comb in grease-proof paper.'

'Her lips trembled like mad,' I said. 'She threw the comb down – little madam.'

I smiled at my wife. Those little spaghetti straps she wore suited her. They showed off the straightness of her shoulders.

'And the time Cwm was ill,' Nerys said.

'Equine flu, wasn't it? She thought she was ill too, didn't she? You tried to give her some medicine, but she was having none of it. She didn't like the chalky powder on her tongue.'

'And I threw the spoon at the wall,' she said. 'I'm not proud of that.'

Nerys took a sip of water, ladylike and calm. The waiter brought salads piled high on plates. I looked around me. I had to admit the place was classy, all tiger furs and dark, velvet cushions.

'What did you two talk about when I was inside?' I asked her.

'Who? Me and that awful man?'

'No, you and Cara,' I said.

I waited. Nerys speared some salmon, rested a mouthful on her tongue and swallowed.

'She gave me the third degree, of course. Wanted to know – yet again – why I left her. I told her – yet again – I had to try to find my feet far away from the farm. Make a success of what I wanted to do.'

'So, she's still cross?'

Nerys shifted in her seat.

'No, I wouldn't say so. She's a pussycat really, compared to me, compared to you, but *I'm* still mad with her.'

'?'

'For being kicked out of college, you clot. What a stupid thing to do.'

We both ate quietly. My tuna steak was rubbery, but I was hungry.

'Ach, never mind, let's talk about us,' I said. 'Is there anything else I should know?'

Nerys looked at me.

'Not just at the moment. I've had a few lucky escapes, you might say.'

'Oh?'

Nerys blew her lips hard and shook her head.

'Cara hasn't told you, then?'

'Told me what?'

I had to admit, I was a convincing liar. Occasionally, I enjoyed acting, especially away from home. Holidays were an excellent excuse to flex my improvisational skills.

'Rupert was the most serious for a while, I guess. But he was crazy.'

'The Scientologist?'

Nerys laughed. Damn. Rumbled.

'So, you want the scoop from the horse's mouth?'

She bit her lip. I leaned in.

'Ay, if you like.'

'Right then. So you know all about the car?'

'The car?'

'The mysterious, red sports car. It's noisy on my street. I'd go to the window to see what was going on. People watch, you know, that type of thing. Might just have been a feeling. Anyway, down there on the street, clear as day, a red sports car.'

'Who was it? Weird how he – did he see you?'

'He must have.'

'Rupert?'

'Ah, you see, my point is Rupert had a lot of money. A hell of a lot of money. People like that, they know people.'

'So it wasn't Rupert behind the wheel?'

Nerys frowned. But I didn't get it. Why send a driver to spy on her?

'Did he think you were having an affair?'

I waited.

'No. More sinister than that.'

'Eh?'

Nerys downed the rest of the glass. I looked around for the waiter. I topped her up myself. I had to oil the machine.

'Flip me sideways, hon,' she said. 'Do you not know anything?'

'?'

'Scientologists, they stick together if you know what I mean.'

I wasn't sure I did.

'It's like a cult,' she said. 'It's not like joining the church. It's more like joining the Fascist party. They don't like defectors.'

'So you were one. A Scientologist?'

'Don't be daft,' she said. 'But I was going with Rupert. That was enough to make him think I was in the club with him. You know, he used to treat me to sushi?'

'Right?'

I topped her up again.

'Not the type of sushi you buy in those little boxes. No, he'd ring up and they'd bring it over. Covered the whole of his table with the stuff. Salmon, raw tuna. There was no way we could eat it all. Then, he started complaining about my feet.'

I looked down at her feet. They looked perfectly fine to me.

'Said they were smelly. Used to ask me to wash them as soon as I walked in the door. There was a wet room just inside the hall.'

'And did you?'

'Uh-huh.'

Nerys ate some more, but I wasn't hungry. I bit into a cherry tomato; it splattered on my shirt.

'Money talks.' I said.

'Then, he asked if I wanted a boob job.'

'A what?'

'Said he'd pay for it. If I wanted one.'

'You didn't, did – '

'Of course I didn't. You've seen for yourself. You must have noticed it's *au naturel* down there.'

Playfully, Nerys waved her fork in front of her chest. I cut a chunk of tuna and pushed it around my plate.

'They're perfect as they are,' I said, and I meant it.

'But you know, I suppose they're not as pert as they were.'

I didn't have what Rupert had. I'd never had his kind of money, or could ever hope to have. It was true: my wife's breasts weren't as north-facing these days – but you know, I was a grown-up man with priorities. My wife lived behind her breasts, not in front of them. Jeez.

'Did that make you angry when he said that? That he was judging you like that?'

'Oh yeah. I gave him his marching orders pretty soon after – but not *because* of that.'

'No?'

'No.'

'Why, then?'

The waiter came over. I asked him to bring more wine.

''Cos of his friends, Duff. They wanted me in The Cult. That's what I called it. That's what it was. A Cult. Pressure. I knew they wouldn't be happy. Rupert wouldn't be happy unless I was in deep. And he *did* have a lot of friends. Important people in the town. People who knew people. Then, these people, they knew more people. Muck spreads.'

I blinked away my disgust. The place sounded screwed for sure.

'Oh, they're everywhere, Duff. Come on. Wouldn't mind betting there's a fair few in Swansea these days.'

My head fizzed. I'd been mixing my pills with hard drink, and I regretted it. I pressed my feet into the floor but the boards felt light, like sponge. I took a deep breath and coughed. Nerys topped up my water.

'And your rag-trade merchant, Tarquin, was it?'

'Taryn. Nothing to tell.'

'No?'

'No.'

'Did he know Rupert?' I asked

'Know him?'

My wife laughed, but it was a fake kind of laugh.

'That's how I met Rupert,' she said.

She flicked her spaghetti straps with her fingers and grinned.

'So, Taryn,' I said. 'Was he one too?

'No, he wasn't. And he thought Rupert was a prick, obviously.'

'*Obviously.*'

'He just had to be nice to Rupert, because Rupert knew people. Other powerful people. It's complicated,' she said.

I thought it through for a moment. So, she had jumped Taryn, a *comparitively* okay-ish bloke, for a mad Scientologist. Even in my sedated state, this didn't make sense to me. Unless of course, it was plain, old-fashioned money she was after. I shook my head.

'What's up?' she asked. 'Look, Duff, you did ask.'

'It's not that,' I said.

'Then, what? Duff – power, of course. He knew people. That's how I got my job.'

I rubbed my face. So, my wife had been prepared to sell her soul to the Devil merely for a job. I thought for a moment.

'But if Rupert sorted you out a plum job, he could un-get you a plum job too?'

'He could,' she said, 'and he did. Then, I met Sabina.'

'Of course, the lesbian.'

My wife watched me. I felt sure she was able to hear my brain ticking. Finally, she finished eating and pushed her plate away. I forced a mouthful of food down. Coming to life between my legs, my dick pulsed, like an angry eel. Nerys smirked.

'Don't think I don't know what you're after,' she said, 'and look hon, you can forget it. I'm not titillating you.'

A foot rubbed my crotch, a playful, light touch. I grinned. Swiftly, she pulled her foot back. Okay, I thought, so the lesbian story can wait. I suggested we head upstairs.

'Wait a minute,' she said, 'I want a pud. You know how I love my puds.'

But I left her to finish her meal alone and went up to our room to greet the drizzle that dusted in through the open window. It was tranquil on our Holy Island. The water rippled in the distance. Tiredly, I lay down on the bed. My lids scraped my eyeballs, like sheets of thin metal.

Nerys nudged me. Her hair smelt of sand. I wondered if she'd been out already, or perhaps she'd popped her head out of the window to breathe in the morning air.

'What's up?' I asked her.

'I don't know,' she said. 'Well, it's just a – I mean – God, Duff, you ask a lot of questions, I just think this time we really do need to get moving.'

Outside in the car park, I breathed in the cleansing, damp air. There were few places I could be in Britain better for my lungs – what's more we were among the bird-fanciers and the folky throw-backs, and this soothed me. I felt as if my feet were buried in the ground.

I looked down to my sandaled toes, sleeping white slugs. What I could use was a shot of that burning sun, Malaga or the Costa-lottas. I had heard the sun was quite the thing. Maybe next year.

So, I tailed behind Nerys, dragging both of our bags behind me. Hers was the heaviest. I wondered what the hell she had in there. We approached the van. Lazily, I looked it up and down. There were waves of salt splattered down the door on the driver's side. I saw a paper docket wedged under the wipers.

'We can't have a parking ticket here, surely,' I said. 'It's a hotel car park for Christ's sake.'

Nerys pulled it out and read it. I waited. She crumpled her face.

'What is it? How much is it?'

'What?'

'How much is it? What's the damage? Can't be that bad?' I snatched the note from her. She looked at me with her eyes more green than hazel. I read.

Thirsty, are you? Hungry, are you? A lot of miles. A lot of dough. So, what do you say? Wanna meet?

'Weird,' I said.

'Yep.'

I spun around and looked for signs of kids loitering, but there was nobody else around.

'So what's it all about?' I asked.

She scrunched the paper into a ball and threw it to the ground.

'Beats me,' she said.

I picked it up and unravelled it. I studied the soft curve of the S's, and the tail of the G's. I scrunched it and threw it. We watched it buffer past the parked cars down to the sand.

'Who would leave such a note?' Then, I spotted a familiar mint Peugeot parked outside the lines. 'Jesus. I don't believe it,' I said.

'Who is it?' my wife asked, her chin shaking.

'Winterson, who else?' I said.

Winterson got out of his car. We dived in the van.

'Surprise, surprise,' Nerys said, settling behind the wheel. 'Will you just look at the state of him?' She turned to me. 'Well, aren't you going to open the door on your side?'

I thought about it. That would have made sense – but ah, there was nothing else for it, Winterson had us trapped. My only alternative was to ask Nerys to drive off, but there was no gust in our engine, and I didn't want to make him angry.

'I'll do it, then,' Nerys said, and she swung her door wide.

Winterson traipsed over – and I *mean* traipsed, but I saw at least he'd changed his clothes. Gone were the candy-stripes and thin shirt, and he'd replaced them with red trousers and a black jumper. His belly flapped over his zip. I could barely digest the sight.

'Nice of you to leave us a note,' I shouted.

'Wha's that?'

'The note,' I said. 'You know. The one you left.'

'Hop on in,' Nerys said.

I could have hissed in her ear. Now we'd never get shot of him. We listened to him lumber round the back and as he did so, he thumped the van. We jumped. With a creepy smile, he appeared at my door. Hesitantly, I unlocked it. He climbed in. He smelt bad, like mouldy Camembert and pound-store body spray. Nerys coughed. Winterson eased himself into the leather and looked down at his lap, then around him, anywhere but directly at us. Winterson's eyes saw: coats slung over the seats; my notebook on the carpet at my feet; a mess of paraphernalia scattered in the back.

'I hate this place,' he spluttered. 'Holy Island, they call it. Scares the shit out of us. Where we headin'?'

I laughed at the cheek of him.

'Where's your beautiful daughter, anyways?'

'Were you hoping to see her?' Nerys asked. 'Too bad, but she says to say hi, and thanks again for everything.'

She patted my knee. Great, I thought, that's just great.

'What about your car?' I asked Winterson. 'You just gonna leave it there like that?'

'Eh? Ar, I'll pick it up tonight, don't worry, Duffy. I fancy a bit of a cruise.'

I decided he was irreversibly broken, positively unhinged. I held a tissue to my nose and pretended to blow. Nerys edged off. Luckily, the tide was out and we headed down towards the road that would lead us back to the mainland. Nerys wore a half-smile. There were times when her kindness meant nothing to me.

'Now, look,' I said. 'We won't be coming back this way again.'

'No probs, don't you worry your pretty head about that. I'll thumb a lift. S'fucken easy. Everyone stops for me.'

He threw me a toothy grin that was hard not to admire. There was quite a gap between his incisors, you could ram a knife in there and give it a wee jiggle. He pulled out a bag of humbugs and offered us both one. I unwrapped one for Nerys. She snatched it from me and threw it in her mouth, like a hungry teenager.

'So, where were we?' Winterson asked.

'?'

'What were we sayin' before – the other night? Remember Brian Blackwell? I liked him a lot.'

'I didn't,' I said. 'He was a prick. Tried to put me down in front of Saul. That was his thing. He tried to make himself look – '

'Saul?'

'My boss, you met him – the conference – remember?'

'Ah, that bloke in the naff trilby? Yeah s'fucken terrible business.'

'What is?'

'All that trouble with his wife.'

'The note,' I said again. 'Did you leave a note on the windscreen?'

'Nope.'

For a moment we all seemed to be lost in confusion, together but apart. This was a mess, a spaghetti junction of WHAT THE FUCK IS GOING ON? And I wondered what it was I felt for Winterson: Sorrow? Misplaced loyalty? Sheer contempt? None seemed sufficient.

'It wasn't your friend, then?' Winterson asked.

Nerys looked at me.

'My friend?'

Now Winterson looked mad.

'The car park by the bar,' he said. 'Your friend in the *hat*.'

Nerys sped the van down the slope. I knew I had to get rid of Winterson, there had to be a way. So I rubbed my keys in my pocket – why? Don't ask me. What the hell would *you* have done? I needed to get my thoughts in order.

Then, with Lindisfarne behind us, we coasted for a while. With a fresh determination, Nerys drove north without any help from me. We reached a dead spot, all tall trees and untrodden turf. I slapped my palm on the windscreen.

'Stop the van,' I yelled.

'Why?' my wife said, a little too calmly for my liking.

'Are you crazy?' I said. 'Look at the view! The sun is high, it's a cracker. Come on, everyone – out! Let's go for a walk.'

Nerys hummed. Only Nerys could substitute a grunt for a hum, but she stopped the van the second I willed it the hardest. High on pills, I decided I could float around the parkland. Jerkily, I nudged Winterson. He got out and took the lead, like this daisy-strewn turf was his own back yard.

We loped behind the great lump, following him in the direction of the trees. Nerys held my hand.

'Well, I will say the wet mud smells lush,' Nerys said.

Winterson trudged his size 11s down in the dirt. They made a dull thud. We walked on. Under gloomy trees, he kicked at puffballs. They coughed their filthy spores right up into our nose hairs.

'Curry powder, that's what they are,' he said.

Nerys corrected him.

'They're poisonous, you daft sod. Stop kicking them, will you? Duff's lungs can't take it. What's his name again?' she hissed.

'Who? Dan,' I told her.

I didn't have a clue which way to turn, but I figured plans were for cowards. Plans were devised by the type of bloke who never entered woodland with twisted ex-colleagues. Except I wished I had one, even a kind of one. To add to matters, I was dizzying up again, fighting down the impulse to hurl. Earlier, I'd known the risks. Just the one, I'd told myself, that's it, for the kicks. I'd popped another pill down.

'Jesus, Dan. Listen to her, will you? She said stop kicking them.'

They smelt disgusting. I clasped my hand around my neck but it only made my breathing worse. Winterson stopped. He turned around and looked sadly at us both.

'Sorry,' he said. 'Very bad of me.' He slapped his own wrist. 'Won't do it again. Sorry, Nerys. Sorry, Duff.' There was a beat. We waited. 'Cara back home then?' he asked, and then walked on. We stayed close behind him.

'Ay,' I said to his back. 'We paid her off.'

Winterson swung around.

'You did what?'

'Only kidding,' I said.

Winterson didn't appear to like my kidding.

'She's fucked a lot of men?'

'Pardon?' I asked.

I dared not look at Nerys.

'S'fucken too much, man. Told me all about it, she did, like I wanted to hear *that*. S'fucken liberty, little tease. Nothing but a filthy prick tease, that one.'

This was unprecedented, even by Winterson's standards. I had to do something.

'Okay,' I said. 'I've seen enough puffballs. It's same old, same old. C'mon, let's turn back.'

'What's the problem? What – you're saying you don't get this all the time? She's a fresh 'un, that one. Bet she's had a fair few. Wouldn't mind betting your whole village has had a go. Fuck all to do round your way, Duff. Winding me up like that. Yeah, they tell me about girls like her.'

I risked a glance at Nerys. Her fury darkened to bug-eyed panic. We stood facing in a triangle. The light was dim. I could see the tree bark, all swirls and warty lumps. I kicked at bark chippings at my feet. Why hadn't Nerys chaperoned Cara? She should have been with her the whole time.

'When did Cara say all this?' I asked Winterson.

Winterson stood with his legs apart, his hands on his hips.

'She would have fucked me too, given the chance. I'm tellin' ya.'

I wanted to laugh. I wasn't even sure Cara enjoyed doing it with Daryl. I wasn't sure *anyone* would enjoy doing it with that spidery goon. This was all too much for Nerys.

'Fuck a porky fatso like you? Are you serious, honey? Would you just look at yourself?'

'Steady, Dan,' I said. 'Simmer down? Not gentlemanly, is it?'

'Nah, your wife's probably right. Can't imagine anyone would wanna do me. Look at this.'

And he lifted his jumper to reveal an almighty pair of sand mounds. He clasped his palms over them and gave them a jiggle.

'They're ample, fair play,' Nerys said.

'Shit for brains too. S'fucken bad enough being skint, but when you look like this – well, Christ, it's torture, you know?'

He looked strange staring at us like that, his pig-eyes lost in the pork fat, but I wasn't fooled by his hang-dog jowls or the flash of contrition sweeping across his face. We had a volatile madman on our hands. We were a good ten minutes from the van and we had to get back, with or without Winterson. So, I decided to do just that. Boldly, I slipped my arm through Nerys's. We turned our back on him. I felt sick, my nerves were shot, but – Bam! I threw up right there on my shoes. I waited for some reprieve but, no, it kept on coming. Like a crazy person, I sprayed acid chunks into a waxy bush. Nerys patted my back.

'Take it easy, man,' Winterson said. 'Summat I said?'

'You could say that,' I said with a new hardness.

'Listen, will you? Please?'

Nerys turned around.

'Promise to behave, then? Only, we're not fooled. We can see right through you... Dan Winterson.

And, at this, he bent down and picked a daisy, one of the few peeping up through the grass.

'Here, for you, petal,' he said, and handed it to Nerys.

'That's not enough, Dan,' Nerys said. 'I want the whole garland. I want to wear it in my hair, like a gypsy queen.'

What the – ? So here we were, with the chance to go back, and Nerys had pulled the brakes on my plan. I wondered about my wife at times. Winterson flopped down on the grass. He tried to cross his legs, but settled instead for making a cumbersome V-shape. He leaned forward, picking more daisies. Concentration transformed his face.

'Should be enough here,' he said. 'Your head's only small.'

'That's the idea,' Nerys said. 'That's the way. There, put your nail through. No, the stem, that's it.'

She sat down next to him and crossed her legs. I joined them.

'That's it,' she said, 'then you – God, Dan, sort it out. Yeah, that's the way, then you thread.'

Winterson's pudgy fingers worked on in silence but, in a short time, Nerys had her garland, and Winterson believed he had made a friend.

Fortunes come, and fortunes go. The French say *le petit bonheur*. Moments of happiness are just that: flashes of fun, but they soon vanish. The trick is to enjoy them while they last. I had the distinct feeling time was running out for me and Nerys. I was no further along in my mission to woo her. The fact remained I owed Angharad two months' wages. To add to matters, I wasn't even sure I *had* a job. My parents were long dead. I had no living siblings. As the mournful song goes, I was a motherless child – broke, unloved and desperate.

Alone in the van, I sensed the floor of the van quivering, pushing up through my feet. Long streaks of light blinded my view, flagging up stubborn blim-holes in the leather. *Saucy, pedantic wretch, go chide late school children.* But I couldn't remember the next line of John Donne's aubade, a poem I once knew by rote. I had come to accept I was getting on.

Nerys's mother had died a long while back. She was with us one minute, and then she was gone. And so it goes. But I was sure it was her death that had sent Nerys loopy for a while. It was not long after her death that she left me.

Slowly, I pulled my faded blue jeans up higher around my waist, the same jeans I'd slept in, the same jeans I'd left Swansea in. With my frayed sleeve, I wiped spray from the windscreen and scanned the scene before me. There was a hardware shop selling gloss paints and cream fridges. In the next shop along there were *po-faced mannequins in A-line dresses.*

I watched my wife eating with Winterson in the café. *Would you call it bonding?* I watched Nerys punch Winterson's arm. She delivered a sharp, right hook. *Some force!* She threw her head back. I could almost hear her trademark honking laugh. The waitress brought them sandwiches. Winterson devoured the lot, like it was his last supper. Nerys picked at her salad, as Nerys does.

A feeble drizzle. The cocoon of the lavender-fresh van. This Winterson thing: it was merely a game Nerys had concocted to try and make me jealous. I was sure of it. My eyes smarted and I rubbed them. Slowly, they paid up and left the café. Winterson was a dog at her heel. When they drew nearer, I put away my notebook and coughed. They stood by my open window.

'Dan was just telling me – now listen to this, hon. It's far out, that's what it is. He once set fire to a Rugby Club!'

'Oh ay?'

'By accident,' Winterson added.

Nerys laughed, a real foghorn. Dan looked full-faced and satisfied.

'That's nothing to be proud of though – surely?' I said. 'Anyone get hurt?'

'No, no,' Nerys said. She looked serious for a second. 'It wasn't his fault – well, it kind of was, but no – it was the boy he was with.'

'Oh ay?'

'Never mind him,' Winterson said proudly. 'Last I heard of him he was dead. Posted overseas he was. Careered right off the road in Norn' Ireland.'

I looked down to his feet and his toenails peeping through his sandals. They were actually curling.

'Duff?' my wife said.

'Hmm?'

'What do you think to that, then?'

'So what? I did too,' I said, rubbing my knees, fighting the temptation to lean across and start the engine myself.

'Did what?' They asked together, like buddies in the playground.

'Set fire to a bush. Down an alley. Not sure why. Something to do. We had a lighter. The owner came out all arms waving. There was a petrol can in his shed. Could have been nasty. Had we seen who done it? I suppose Gareth and me, we didn't look the type. We looked like nice boys.'

But Winterson didn't look keen to have his story trumped and he hauled himself over to my side. He lumbered in and I budged up. A lighthouse blinked sluggishly in the sea mist. Gulls swooped low. Winterson smiled to himself. His presence was another victory won at my expense.

We pulled up next to a van selling coffee. Winterson had spotted an adventure playground on the other side of the road. Excitedly, he flew over. From the van, we watched him crouch over a wobbly bridge, then swing on a rubber tyre with a vacant expression on his face. Nerys laughed and finally went to fetch him.

Whatever had pulled Winterson in our direction, it hadn't been me.

I knew if we were to rid ourselves of him, I would need to change tactic and fast. So I decided to try the silent treatment and bore him in to submission. I figured it shouldn't be too difficult with my energy levels as low as they were. When we set off again, I listened to Nerys twittering away to him – about Cara, Daryl, her multiple attempts to learn to drive and the time she crashed into the test centre wall.

Ten whole minutes passed before Nerys nudged me. I heard a flustered whisper in my ear. Forcefully, she dug her knuckles into my knee.

'Duff, help me out here, will you?'

Not that Winterson seemed to notice.

His beef with me was now a mere slither of salami, soon it would be nothing at all. I imagined what it would be like to be alone with my wife again, sat idly on deckchairs, sipping wine. I could almost feel the tiny ants skipping across my feet – tickling, tickling.

Nerys slowed the van in a country lane and pulled over under a line of birches. The van had never looked so conspicuous, moored at the gates of a mansion. From his bag, Winterson pulled out a pack of cards.

'?'

'Dan's promised me a tarot reading,' Nerys said. She turned off the engine.

'What, here?' Nervously, I looked around. 'What if someone comes?'

'Relax.' Nerys said. 'You're always so uptight.'

So, Winterson shuffled a deck that was all swirling moons and puckered crones. He laid the cards out on the dashboard and asked Nerys to choose ten. She did so.

'No, use your left hand, that's it. You have to use the hand you don't normally use.'

He pulled an amethyst from his pocket and rubbed it along the top of Nerys's pile.

We watched him flip them over one by one. I wanted to laugh. Winterson spoke like he was speaking in tongues. The information seemed to come from somewhere else, not from him. A good trick, I thought, a convincing one. He spoke of a recent spell, long and lonely, shortly to end. I laughed out loud. My wife glared at me.

'Don't mind him,' Nerys said to Winterson. 'He's a typical moon in Taurus.'

My wife soaked up every word, like it meant something.

'You next,' Nerys said to me.

'No, thanks,' I said.

Winterson waded in. 'Go on, what you afraid of?'

But I kept my head down and scribbled in my pad. *All this, just because I bedded your mad girlfriend – once. Ruby wasn't worth it; she wasn't worth all THIS.*

Suddenly, Winterson simmered down until he said nothing at all. Now, I understood Nerys had conquered Winterson and as it turned out it was the best thing she could have done. He had wanted a challenge, but with our new friendly stance, we no longer offered him one. We had worn him down.

Keep in touch, I said, when our faux-chummy fists parted in the lay-by. *Hmm*, he said, which made me think it was the last thing he would have wanted. We left him thumbing a lift. Cars thrashed past, but they didn't stop.

My mother had sent me to Ampleforth for a while, until the money ran out. I was there for two years, struggling through my exams, trying to keep up with the toffs. There'd been a man there who liked to coax me into the woods. The priests at Ampleforth had voiced their disapproval many times, warning me to keep away – *ah, those dark priests. Forgive me Father, for he's not a murdering gypsy, he let me play on his uke. No, really, Father.*

He'd read the cards for me. I remembered one card in particular. It had been all swords and daggers. Swords represented all I was about to leave behind, he told me – or at least I think that's what he said. I recalled there had been the Death card. Such was my luck. I'd heard about death; it didn't sound the kind of thing I'd be interested in. *Flesh becomes bones, bones become dust, and then you're nothing.* The priests had been right about that, at least.

Brown road signs flashed past and we carried on up to Edinburgh.

'So, you're telling me, you came away after being in hospital, then you were taken in again, and you're still doing this thing?'

'That's right,' I said with a grin.

He sat opposite us. We scanned his brown eyes as they searched for sense. He was neat, straight up, 6ft and a fag paper. Gay? The side parting was a possible indicator, although it didn't appear to be me he was interested in.

We'd met him an hour earlier in a bookshop – a bookshop

he just so happened to own. We'd watched him approach us with his chin forward and his briefcase held before him, like a treasured metal detector. He'd looked different to the others we'd so far encountered, so I'd invited him to join us for a drink.

I noticed in the fifteen years since my last visit, Edinburgh had weathered well. It had become a little singed around the edges, perhaps, with the passing of time, but I was enamoured with the place all over again. I liked the bar we found ourselves in. The air smelt of warm whisky. There were a handful of early drinkers dotted around my line of vision. The magnificent castle was visible from the toilet window.

'Are you trying to kill yourself?' he asked with a candour that made our eyes widen. 'You seem to be going the right way about it.'

Nerys listened and painted on her half smile. Calmly, she stroked the inside of her elbow.

'He's determined,' Nerys said. 'Once he sets his mind on something.'

Yes, I thought, yes *exactly* that.

'But what about your daughter? The farm? It's a lot for a wee kid to handle – no? What with drugs too. Will she be okay?'

I studied him. He had the pallor of someone who spent too long on the Internet. His face was supported by a square jaw, all deep cleft and six-o'clock shadow. Hang on, I thought. Rewind a second. I'm not the type of bloke you take me for. I'm not a *bad* person.

'Philip, he said, holding out his hand. 'I haven't even told you my name. Philip Marchant.'

He had quite a grip for a slender man.

'Nerys Winterson,' my wife said. 'And this here is Duff.'

Nerys Win–? So Nerys wanted a bit of fun. Fine.

'Oh?' he said. 'You don't meet many Duffs.'

'Here in Scotland, it means the dark one,' I said.

Carefully, he placed his briefcase by his feet. He kept his hand on it.

'I know what it means. So, your daughter, how old is she?'

'Nineteen,' I said. 'Nineteen and three quarters.'

'Just – it's a bit selfish – no? To leave her when she sounds like she's in trouble.'

I crossed my arms. So, he was one of the repressed, defensive types I was clever at spotting. Marchant personified the snippy-when-challenged sort. They walked among us, his type, you just had to watch your back. *So then, Philip Marchant, impress us. You obviously want to dazzle us with your knowledge of – what? Local history? Literature nobody reads? Go!*

'Duff?' My wife tapped my hand. 'Put your pen down, will you? Just said I'm taking Philip outside to show him the van. We'll be right back.'

My lungs heaved, water-logged. I watched them go, my wife small and ballsy by his side. I took a moment to breathe. My eyes were dry and itchy, the fault of the morphine again, maybe. The truth was I felt less of a man, more like half a man, half a world away – what's more I wasn't sleeping. I was as dead-eyed as last night's fish supper.

Lately, I suffered moments of nausea that either passed

gently on by, or pushed up into my burning throat. My stomach was like a popcorn machine. My mind drifted in and out of Nerys's thoughts, in and out of my own. And here we were in Scotland closing in on Aberdeen, the place where it would all be resolved one way or another. The question of Nerys and me, I wondered if it would work itself out. Within a matter of days, my wife's flight would take off as scheduled back to Santa Fe. Would she be on it?

And if she did agree to stay with me, what would she be missing out in Santa Fe? What was there for a smart chick like Nerys in that comedy town? After work, a ten-minute circuit in the gym. Don't work too hard though, need to keep up the boho façade. And in the evening? A sip of whisky, a DVD alone while batting away unwanted calls from the likes of Taryn, Rupert and The Lesbian – and oh, look, there's Rupert's friend in his sports car again – *C'mon everybody, wave to the nice man.*

I chewed on my pen and looked around me. A German couple sat at the bar nursing a single rum between them. The sweet, spicy smell wafted my way. When in Rome – no? So, my lungs and me, we took to the bar. I plumped for a Mai Tai. *This is nice. This is sophisticated. This is the type of thing you do on holiday.* I tasted it. Not too sweet. Marchant returned with my wife.

'Well, blow me,' he said. 'It's certainly retro.'

He twirled my blue cocktail umbrella with those slender fingers of his.

'Now, tell me, Duff, what kind of thing do you like to read? Do you have the time?'

'Hunter S Thompson,' I said, a little too quickly. It was the only writer I could pluck from the recesses of my mind. 'He's the man.'

Marchant smiled, but I didn't like the intent behind it.

'A farmer with a taste for the hard stuff, eh?'

Not *just* a farmer, thank you. I could trip you up with New German Cinema any day of the week, Marchant.

'You like film, Philip?'

'Ay, world cinema,' he said.

'Fassbender or Wenders? Which do you prefer?'

C'mon quickly, man, quickly. I heard his tongue click.

'Both German. Same time. Same place,' he mocked a yawn. 'Very *very* different, though. A lazy comparison – no?'

'No,' I said.

'Alright, then, Fassbender,' he said.

Ah, so he was gay.

Marchant's flat looked habitable enough: a computer at a desk; white, dust-free bookshelves; freshly-cut lilies, sweet to the nose. There was a touch of filigree about the place, neat little touches that fuelled my suspicion. There was a walking cane with a turquoise handle, a hat stand with a panama, a trilby, a mohair beret... it was the kind of place you'd call a home if you had Marchant's kind of money. So, I did what I always did in unfamiliar territory, I disappeared to take a nose around the bathroom.

Edinburgh was a fine city; I'd always thought so. It wasn't

London, where the real movers and shakers lived, but it was a decent pot shot at Being Vital, nonetheless.

Back in the living room, I went to the window. Across the way, long shadows floated above the paving, and I leaned out for a better view. The gritty air rinsed my face and swept past my ears. Across the road, in a neat little square, there were dandelions. I liked dandelions but I'd never seen them as weeds. I'd always suspected the real weeds were walking and talking among us.

'Careful, you'll fall,' Marchant said, and he grabbed my leg. He behaved like a damn rugby pro. I stumbled back onto the polished floor.

'What time will she be back?' Marchant asked, a touch too keenly.

'Who, Nerys? An hour or so, I guess. Don't mind her. She'll be spending money I can't afford. You know how it is.'

'Something I said?'

Nope, it's not all about you, sunshine.

'I don't think so,' I said.

An hour earlier, Nerys had insisted on wandering the city by herself, but that had been fine by me; that was just the kind of thing she liked to do. Coming here to Marchant's flat had been Nerys's idea. I would have preferred to have slept in the van. Nonetheless, I wasn't one to turn down a bath, a free drink, and the chance to sit back on a leather couch. I did so. Marchant handed me a long-stemmed glass. I guzzled the red down and handed the empty glass back to him.

'Kind of you to have us over,' I said.

'A pinot noir,' he said.

'Thought so.'

'Not the expensive stuff.'

'No.'

He took the armchair and spread those long arms of his wide. He looked like he was recovering from a punishing sprint. I tapped my knees. My head spun. I could use another drink.

'Make yourself at home,' Marchant said.

'You like it here?'

'Ay, have a life here, friends, projects,' he said.

'Oh ay?'

'Yip.'

I waited and waited, and waited.

'What kind of thing keeps you busy?' I asked.

'Well now, I arrange a lot of festivals up here.'

He sat up and tapped his chin, then slid his finger across that deep cleft of his. *Och ay, you're important, Marchant, I get it.*

'But now and again... well, it takes up too much of my time.'

'Been doing a bit of writing myself,' I confessed.

'I can see.'

I put down my pen and immediately regretted opening up that little arena for discussion. Marchant raised his eyebrows as if to say *you want me to take a look?* I suspected he'd hate for me to showcase my juvenilia.

'Just private, stream-of-consciousness stuff, really. You wouldn't – '

'Well, you have to start somewhere.'

'Indeed.'

There was a beat, then another. I wondered whether he had a boyfriend tucked away somewhere in the city. The flat reeked of coupledom. There had been a waft of coconut and almond in the bathroom that made me pine for the feminine touch. It had been brimming to the rafters with creamy unguents in tall bottles with wooden stoppers. There had been muslin face cloths piled neatly on a chair.

Marchant stood up. The top of his head skimmed the light-fittings. Slowly, he filled my glass with more wine. I sipped.

'Nerys and me, we're being followed,' I said. 'I'm sure of it.'

I didn't know why I felt compelled to share this, but there was no-one else to tell.

'Why?' he asked, pulling gently on his thumb. 'What is it you've done?'

He sat back down and leaned forward. *Now* I was interesting. I looked at him properly. Marchant was an odd sock. He had the demeanour of someone who needed quiet routine, otherwise he'd implode. I took another sip. The place was oddly still and I willed him to put on some music. Both of us needed to loosen up a little.

'Why?' he asked again. 'Are you in trouble?'

Before I could answer, he hauled himself up and headed out the door. There was the sound of rustling and I wondered where he'd got to. Fine, then, I would just have to put some music on myself. So, I rose up and pressed the round button on the walnut radio. Radio 3. I turned the volume down. Opera it would have to be.

I could not deny there was something disquieting about my host, but not in a bad way, more in a way that intrigued me. He was unfamiliar to me, insofar as I was unfamiliar with his type. At The Faculty, there were a few like Marchant, but back there, there had been a relaxed air and the type of atmosphere where we could fool around a little. Until, that is, I heard what they'd been saying about me. Then, it wasn't funny anymore.

With my host, I knew I would have to work a bit harder. I would need to scramble around in my fuzzy brain for some common ground. Marchant returned, gripping a trophy.

'What's this?' I asked.

Gently, he sat in his chair and resumed his dead star posture. I slumped down on the sofa.

'What's a typical day for you then, Duff?'

At home? At work? What, man, what?

'Tell me, what do you do there at The Faculty?'

Ah, so it was only The Faculty that interested him. I suspected a humble small-holding wouldn't be enough to pique his interest.

'I don't work every day,' I said without apology.

'Oh.'

'Tuesdays are busy. That's the Big One for me. I start with an hour of Cognitive Psychology. An hour of paperwork. But the afternoon's the thing. I dive straight in with Italian Cinema.'

'So you're a renaissance man?'

I coughed, knowing I'd have to slow my drinking. The wine slipped down my throat too easily.

'And yourself?' I asked.

He gave me the trophy to handle. I read the inscription.

Under 18s Snooker Champion, Edinburgh 1974.

'Would you rather a lager, Duff?'

'No, wine's good.' I changed my mind. 'Yes, a lager will be great.'

He went out to fetch me one. I shouted after him.

'You the regional champ, then?'

But I waited a long time for him to return, and I didn't want a lager, not really. He strode back in and sat down.

'It's a passion, bordering on obsession,' he said. 'The counting, the colours, the wobble of the net when the ball shoots in. Hurtling down the green. It's a glorious game. Focus and precision. That's what you need.'

He flexed his mighty fingers. Eyeing the delicate, fluted vase by my side, he demoed a pot-shot. He reached into his pocket and pulled out a blue chalk.

'This wee bairn. This same chalk. The day of the trophy. Back when I was ten. We took it in turns, my friends and me to host the tournaments. I won, of course, every time. But that didn't stop me. It was the game, not the winning. All about the game.'

It was clear to me Marchant was a bragger, the type I wished I could be if only I had the gall. I noticed he had a scar on his right hand, next to his little finger.

'How did you get that?' I asked nodding.

'Ay, this little thing? Not sure I should say.'

'No?'

He leaned back in the chair.

'No.'

The buzzer rang – thank God. Marchant went to answer it.

My wife entered the room, smiling. She whiffed of jasmine. Slyly, I looked her up and down. There was a slick of banana yellow across her eyelids. Sparkly terracotta was smeared on her cheeks. I wondered if we were off to an Eighties party. I knew what she'd been up to: she'd been to grab all the freebies. She'd had a cheap make-over. Chirpily, she went over to the window. I followed her. Marchant hovered alone by his armchair.

We saw: a dim blanket of gold coating the wet roofs; bare streets with no sign of life; a brown bird perched on a chimney. I saw: the back of her head; a small auburn freckle just below her neck; a woman facing a fork in the road – a woman who just so happened to be my wife. I kissed her hair. So, we were getting somewhere, and in full view of Marchant.

It was getting late and the evening air was growing cold. I flashed my eyes around the room for my jumper.

'Duff?' Marchant looked at my empty glass. I dared not ask for another. I asked for another. As he left the room, Nerys smiled at me.

'Nice, isn't he?' she said.

'Ach, he's okay.'

'I like his straight-up and down-ness, you know?'

But I wasn't so keen. I was already nostalgic for Winterson. At least, like me, Winterson was a maverick.

'So, anyway, what you been up to? Why no goods to show off?'

'Ah, nothing much, hon, you know.'

'Where is it, then?'

'Where's what?'

'The van. Where have you hidden it?'

I felt more protective over my van than ever. At this rate it could be my only home.

'Relax,' she said. 'It's just around the corner. On a nice quiet street with proper houses.' She whispered to me. 'I wanted to park it somewhere safe.'

She clicked her heels on the bare floorboards and headed out the door. I peered out of the window. I had to agree with my wife, there was something strange about this street. Hard to achieve in Edinburgh, but still, there it was. It was a dark strip. The streetlights were in short supply. Even the windows opposite resembled watchful eyes. I watched them light up one by one. They were coming alive and multiplying. I could have been in a Film Noir, or a Graham Greene novel. Not that I'd read any Greene. Not that I'd read much at all for a while. Novels: I didn't have the patience. In truth, I had been too stressed to do much at all.

Nerys returned and smiled at me.

'So, you're not going to tell me?' I asked.

'Tell you what, hon?'

Marchant placed our drinks on the coffee table and sat on the sofa. His eyes looked sad. Nerys sat by his side and patted his knee.

'You okay, hon?'

'I think so,' he said.

Marchant tapped her hand and we watched a tear run down his nose.

'You sure, hon?'

Ah, sweet, kind Nerys.

'My boyfriend left me,' he said. 'Just like that. I woke up one morning and – '

'Oh God,' Nerys said. 'Did he not even leave a note?'

'No.'

'Oh,' my wife said. 'Some people.'

Marchant pulled a freshly ironed handkerchief from his pocket and blew his nose. He took his time about it. I shifted my feet, unsure what to say. I didn't do reassurances, not in the way Nerys was able to, and I decided now would be an opportune time to ask Marchant for that bath he'd offered me in the bookshop. He nodded to the hall. I took my stiff neck with me and left them to it.

As I ran a bath, the thought of my car-crash life pounded in my head until I wasn't sure I could take it anymore. Nothing I touched turned to gold – nothing – and I hadn't reached the age of forty without this realisation in place. It was true: life just kind of *happened* to me. Life didn't so much dance to my tune, as danced on my grave. I wasn't even sure I *had* a tune. If I did, it would be akin to a strangled hum.

I dipped my toe in the bath water. Tepid. I hauled myself in anyway. A sea of bubbles rose to the rim. Picture, if you will, the tub as a frothy pint of Guinness. Roughly, I wriggled my toes against the taps. I lay back and reached down to the floor for my jeans. Manically, my heart banged in my chest. Three solid rasps on my inhaler completed the pleasure. Drowsily, I closed my eyes. I was alive, but only just. Easy does it.

I held my breath and listened to the sound of their voices through the walls. I could hear Nerys's high-pitched coo above his tenor moan. So, Nerys had waited until I was gone to lay her heart bare. I suspected she'd be telling him all kinds of things in there: information I could do with hearing, information that might help me to form a fuller picture of her. There was still so much I didn't know about my wife. Gently, I coughed and opened my eyes. An hour in this aloe vera boudoir, with its seashells and wicker baskets, and they'd soon be banging on the door. Well, they could go hang.

My undulating emotions were hard to pin down. My thoughts were deep one minute and shallow the next. What *was* I feeling? I found this nigh-on impossible to answer. There was a wariness I couldn't put my finger on.

Nerys walked with me in the direction of the van. It rained hard. The stone terraces were sombre and lifeless. It was just after six. Shops were shutting for the day. We passed a bored waiter smoking in a doorway.

Earlier, I'd nodded off listening to Marchant's sonorous voice over lunch. I had tried to listen. After all, the man had been good enough to rustle us both up a salad, but I had resented being held hostage and forced to feign interest in his trophies. Nerys, though, had cooed for the both of us. How to tame a woman like Nerys?

'So what went on in there, exactly?'

'Huh?'

'Don't mess,' I said. 'Last night, when I was in the tub, what was said?'

'Said?'

The rain jagged, it was murderous. We dived under a shop awning and waited. A tramp appeared, reclaiming his cardboard mattress. Gruffly, he demanded we leave immediately. With our eyes down, we walked on, allowing our skin to take a battering.

'Simple,' she said with her head bowed. 'I told him what I did to you – and why I did it. That seemed to do the trick. That cheered him up.'

'And?'

But she didn't answer. Instead, she kept her eyes half-closed in the rain. Her silence didn't fool me. I knew she was playing a game. As we approached the van, I blinked. What? Again? Surely not?

'Another parking ticket. Let me,' I said.

And I swiped the note from the grip of the wipers.

Tired, are you? Need a room? Knock, knock, who's there? Need a friend?

My heart fluttered in my chest. I had to admit there was a certain rhythm to it. So who did we know with rhythm? I swung around, but there was no sign of Winterson – of course not Winterson. Who then? Who?

'The handwriting: it's the same,' I said.

But she didn't seem to hear me. My voice had to contend with a lorry reversing and the hellish crash of a shutter being pulled down. To cap it all, an ice-cream van started up –

Frère-a-Jacques. Nerys shrugged and opened the driver's side. She got in as if this *thing* in my hand *was* a parking fine. And I wondered who was this woman I called my wife? Who was Nerys, exactly? The slightest test ruffled her, yet she didn't appear to sweat the serious stuff.

'Duff,' she mouthed through the windscreen. 'You coming in – or what?'

'What,' I mouthed back.

To calm myself, I willed myself to think of a number. Count back from twenty, I told myself – vingt – dix-neuf – dix-huit. I kept my eyes on Nerys. She started the engine and edged forward. I didn't move. Slowly, I closed my eyes.

My theory was we didn't know people as well as we might like, not even those close to us. What we assumed to be the truth was liable to slip at any second from our grasp. People changed all the time.

I conjured my first girlfriend, Sarah. My image of her was sketchy and half-formed. I wondered if I'd recognise her in the street if I saw her now. In school, she'd worn lop-sided bunches and flat, sensible shoes. She'd dressed her face in a podgy, sluggish smile.

I thought of Ruby and I wondered if she'd kept the shaved head she'd brandished five years ago. As for me, I was sure I had a few less visible markers, fewer eyelashes, upper and lower.

Nerys had changed. She had become a woman of means. Her soul was much the same, of course, but a soul is invisible. You can't display a soul to the casual observer. You need the extra padding. No, I decided if you weren't wandering the streets looking for Nerys, you wouldn't know her. Admittedly, she had the same peachy complexion, the same spun-gold locks, but what of it? Time had proved itself to be little more than a great bottle of turps, wiping over all I'd come to know.

I opened my eyes, and as I did so, the bonnet screeched to a halt inches from my stomach. Well, well, well, so Nerys had needed to play a little trust game.

'Who's following us?' I asked my wife as I settled back in the van.

'Beats me, hon. Why you asking me?'

'Only you don't seem concerned.'

She bit her bottom lip.

'You think it's someone we know?' I asked.

'Well, hon, you do know some strange people. Not that I feel threatened by them. It's just weird, that's all.'

I turned away from my wife and stared out of the window and into the wing mirror. We edged away from the city. I watched passing shops zoom away from me and the skewed perspective made my head rush. Winterson was the oddest person I knew. There had been Ruby too, but I failed to see why she would bay for my blood after all this time, she'd been gone a long time. So, who was left? Angharad, of course, but Cara had said she was in Munich. I rubbed my chin, clueless as to why anyone would go to the trouble of hunting me down. The cost of fuel alone was a hefty investment. I picked up my notebook and pen. *Often I wonder if I'm even*

*here. Gravity! I'm calling you! You should be doing what you're
supposed to be doing, rooting me down with the rest of the human
race.*

'So where we headed?' I asked.

'The water,' she said. 'I want to be by the water.'

Nerys followed the road signs to Leith. Grimly, I took in
the general to-and-fro. Even in the early evening, Edinburgh
struck me as a morning city. It was the kind of city where life
revolved around breakfast. Everywhere I looked there were
dark tables tended by blissed-out waiting staff.

*A pretentious café, Leith. Hockney prints on the wall. Straight lines
and soft edges. I don't –*

I don't think the stalker was on Nerys's mind as she
counted the money in her purse, but with my wife it was
hard to tell what she was thinking. We waited and waited and
waited. Hell, it was a Sunday. Waiting staff were notoriously
tardy on a Sunday.

After some time, our waiter dragged his sleepy eyelids over
to our table. *We get it, sunshine. You're too hip and fabulous for
this job you've been assigned. Well, listen to me, sunshine, serve me.
Today, you're a servant, my servant. I have money in my pocket
and you're going to do as I say.*

'Who you scowling at, hon?'

I ran my fingers up and down my raffia place mat. I
wondered.

'Do you think men are spoilt brats, Nerys?'

'Yep,' she said in a heartbeat. 'Damn right.'

I didn't like this place. I didn't understand the world of restaurants. It was a strange idea, paying to eat in unfamiliar surrounds, being charged for food you could easily grab from the corner shop and eat in the van. Nerys cocked her head to one side. She treated me to a concerned look.

'What's up?' she asked.

But I couldn't answer her. In truth, I didn't know where to begin. Your first love is the hard love, the one that calcifies in your belly and never leaves you. It was *nice* to be here with Nerys, away from Cara and Daryl.

'Why did you do it?' I asked.

She looked at me.

'What's up?'

'Say to Marchant we'd stay the night. I wanted to get cracking. You knew that.'

She blew her lips. Other diners peered over their menus at us.

'Honey, he wanted us to sleep over. He was upset. You saw how he was. Jeez, what could I do? You think I wanted to? Besides, I wanted – I could use a bath.'

She sniffed her arm pits and recoiled, but she smelt sweet enough to me. So, last night I'd wallowed in the bath listening to them. When I wandered back into the living room, I found them sat yards apart. Marchant had gripped his trophy tightly.

Nerys grabbed my place mat.

'Stop *doing* that,' she said.

'Ay! Give it back.'

She placed it back down and smoothed it over.

'So, who is it?' I asked again.

'I told you – I don't – '

'You've told me nothing. Hardly a damn thing.'

'Look, Duff.' She leaned in closer. 'The thing is – oh look, alright.'

'?'

Her phone bleeped. She glanced at the screen. The waiter came back. With a waft of her hand, Nerys shoved a pile of notes in his hand. The boy stared at the money, like all his Christmases had come at once. Casually, she walked out into the street. When I'd gathered enough energy, I ran after her. I broke into a run but I lost my footing and crashed against the wall. I paused to catch my breath. Nerys spun around.

'Come on,' she said. 'Honey please, hurry up, we've got to go.'

Confusion and wonder slapped each other in my head. Was this another one of her games? Run in the opposite direction, my head said. Follow her lead, my heart said. Indulge your sense of adventure. Hell, I was even *excited*.

In the van, she revved up the engine. When the sun broke through the sliding clouds, it turned the sea platinum. We passed a line of restaurants. We headed back in the direction we came – I think –

But no, we changed course and she hurtled closer to the water. Too stunned to speak, I gnashed my teeth together. My jaw stiffened. She slowed and rammed on the brakes.

'Get out,' she said, but I stayed where I was. 'You'll see,' she said. 'You want to know who it is that badly? Then, I'll show you.'

We waited by the van. I kicked at the pebbles and looked out to sea. A gliding yacht melted in the mist. With my tongue weighty in my mouth, I paced up and down the pebbles, in a state of shock. I looked down to my feet. There was an empty can, a ring pull, a floating plastic bag. I heard a crunching sound and I turned to see where Nerys was looking. Slowly, like a sepulchral memory, a woman walked towards us. She had bullish shoulders and long, dark curls.

'Nerys,' she said.

'Sabina.'

So it was Sabina, the lesbian. Nerys leaned back against the van. She bounced her heel off the wheel.

'Good of you to go to all this trouble,' Nerys said.

'Have you got a little something for me in that van of yours?'

Sabina spoke with a voice that was smoky and deep. With her legs wide apart, she stood facing my wife, her hands on her hips.

'No,' my wife said. 'Why should I?'

'Duff Boyd,' I said, reaching out my hand, trying to diffuse the situation, but my hand dangled in the air, untouched.

'What you can do is whistle for it,' Nerys said.

Nerys and Sabina stood in a face-off, breath to breath.

'Sweetie, you screwed me over. Just want what's mine. You know how these things work: I lend you money, you pay it back. Except you didn't. You jumped town and boarded a flight. Just like that.'

I listened and decided I liked Sabina's accent; it was exotic to my ears. I pulled my wallet from my back pocket and looked sadly inside. Sabina laughed.

'Two-hundred thousand dollars,' Sabina said.

I couldn't believe what I was hearing. We were hurtling up to Aberdeen with someone else's money. One hell of an amount.

'Right,' I said. 'I don't know what's –'

'Shut up, Duff,' my wife said. 'Mind your own – you wanted to know who wrote the notes? Well this bitch wrote the notes. She's the loon who's been tailing us.'

Bitch? Loon? Whistle for it? I looked past them to an articulated lorry parked-up by a warehouse. Next to it was the Citroen with the bashed-in bonnet.

Suddenly, Nerys grabbed a chunk of Sabina's hair. Sabina looked weird contorted like that, with her head down in line with my wife's breasts. Sabina tried to wriggle free. Her fist swung towards Nerys's face. I yelped. She looked up to my wife's face, like a dead-eyed method actor about to kill her with her bare hands.

'Shut up,' my wife screamed again. 'Shut up. If you think you can just come here and do what you – you want teaching a lesson.'

Finally, I went right up to the both of them and prised my wife's fist from Sabina's hair. Satisfied, I stood between them with my arms wide, like a football referee, simple and efficient, except I wasn't.

Nerys swerved past me and dived flat on her belly. I flinched. The pebbles would be rough under her skin. She grabbed Sabina's ankles. I stood there, motionless.

'If I don't get my money I'm going straight to the cops,' Sabina said. 'Right here in this town.'

Sabina jiggled her ankle, like she was trying to shake the neighbour's terrier. Eventually, she broke free. Defeated, Nerys got up and hoiked up her jeans. Little rivers of blood seeped down to the hem of her socks.

'You wouldn't dare,' Nerys said.

'Try me.'

I didn't know what to do or say. My wife had revealed herself to be a criminal on the run, and she had the temerity to tear strips from her lesbian girlfriend. Some nerve.

'What are you doing up here, Sab? How much did your airfare cost you? You needn't have bothered buying a ticket. Only here on holiday. I haven't jumped the country. Just needed to get my head together.'

So, the reason my wife had returned had not been to aid to my recovery, as I had willed myself to believe, it had been to escape her girlfriend. I turned away and looked down to the water's edge – where else?

'The business will do great,' Nerys said.

'What have you done with it?'

'Done?'

'The money I gave you. How far have you got setting it all up?' Sabina asked.

'Been drafting a business plan,' my wife said. 'I've been looking into production costs and – '

'Man, that's bullshit,' Sabina said, sitting down on the pebbles. 'I gave you the money ages ago. What the hell have you done with it?'

'I can't just leap in and spend it,' my wife said. 'I have to get the best prices. It's only fair on me, only fair on you.'

Nerys sat beside her. Sadly, I slid back in the van, shut the door and hung my head in my hands. I was as lifeless as the crumpled blazer under my feet. There was no game plan for this unprecedented turn of events – what's more I was too worn out to think straight. I watched them through the salty window. Sabina wiped a tear from Nerys's eye and Nerys licked her girlfriend's finger clean.

Money: what it makes us do to each other, what it makes us do to ourselves. You have it, and you know what money can do, you know its power. I had long concluded only the rich knew money's true worth. For the rich, it was a velvety world of endless parties and tax avoidance. Money was a vehicle to take for a long, Sunday drive. Money was an amusement, a mere pastime.

Sabina didn't look the affluent type. Her pores spewed the sickly scent of cheap patchouli. She wore a students' ying-yang symbol around her wide, porcine neck. If she had walked in to a bar, you would have thought she was a raddled, no-nonsense cab controller with a few tales to tell. Yet my wife owed her a small fortune and she had the temerity to act as if Sabina was dog turd on her shoes.

I wondered how my wife lived over there in Santa Fe that she needed that kind of money. Did she own a fleet of cars? Did she have a ranch in Maine complete with gold-plated horses? Were there silver palm trees in those grounds of hers she rented? Perhaps she had an insatiable coke habit. I could only guess her Moroccan rugs were weaved with precious pearls. I just didn't get it.

So I'm in Marchant's shower, soaping myself raw with vanilla or verbena – or some such. I step out and wrap a giant, fluffy towel around my waist. I look in the mirror. In return, the mirror doesn't look pleased to see me. I smile back at my washed-out, sunken eyes, red with worry. I wonder what happened to the tan I had started to develop. Who was Duff Boyd? It was possible you could take me for a children's entertainer – or a tour guide. If you airbrushed out my freckles, I could pass as a d-list actor. With my square jaw, I could play a gangster with a line or two. Perhaps a stunt double.

What kind of place was Santa Fe? I imagined it was little more than a sleazy toy town. I pictured the main drag in London's King's Cross crossed with Mexico's sunburnt streets. Perhaps it looked a bit like both of these places, the kind of place where you could lose a sense of who you were if you weren't careful. Drowsily, I got dressed and went to join the others.

Marchant wore long, tie-waisted shorts and a neat, lemon shirt. He smiled at the two of them sat together at his dining table, Sabina a stunned rabbit in the headlights, and Nerys a sulky schoolgirl. I recalled his face last night when we'd crashed through his door, each carrying a pack of lagers in our hands. We'd been a mad mob: Nerys with her angry eyes and grazes down her shin, Sabina with her rough complexion turned pink with shame.

Nerys pushed her plate to one side. Hungrily, Sabina hijacked the abandoned potatoes and she ate them, like a woman amplified, a woman fivefold. I watched Marchant kneel down and rub cream into Nerys's grazed shins. *Careful, Maestro, that's my wife's legs you're lavishing with those slender palms of yours.* Sternly, I signalled to my wife – and I felt like a hulking, brooding actor, I tell you: *I want to talk to you outside – alone.* Nerys looked at me with a flicker of contempt – *how inconvenient, how rude of you to commandeer in company. Tough,* I said with my eyes. *Outside now* – wherever outside might have been in a third-floor tenement.

Marchant's communal garden was comprised of square flower beds and pigeon-proof railings. We sat side by side on a bench. The birds sounded angry, a Scottish kind of angry.

'What is it?' she asked me. 'Can't you see how stressful this is for me? Only I'd like a little appreciation of the fact.'

'Oh sure,' I said. 'And who's causing all the stress?' I waited for her to answer but she didn't. She looked up to a starling flying over the rooftops. We both stared down to the quiet road.

'So what is all this?' I asked. 'How are you going to pay her back, anyway?'

'I have the money,' she said. 'And some. I was just testing her.'

'What?'

'I have it all sat in my account. Every penny. See, I'm only doing what she can't do for herself. She's useless. I've got it sitting in my account earning serious interest.'

'Right.'

Nerys sighed.

'See, I wanted to see if she trusted me. And to be honest with you, I'm heartbroken.'

Hearing this from my wife's lips made my own heart sink to my knees.

'I was hoping she was the one for me.'

'But I thought you were just flirting with – '

'That doesn't surprise me, Duff. For you: all these questions, it's just titillation. What about two souls coming together?'

'Do your Mula Bandhas align or something?'

'Our what? Honey, that's absurd.'

But I'd heard enough. I leapt up, stood before her and pulled her up from the bench. Somehow, I managed to drag her out of the gates where the van was waiting.

'What about Marchant, Sabina?' she asked.

'To hell with them,' I said.

In the van, I put my foot down. I glanced at her phone on the dashboard. It was eleven o'clock on a Monday morning. The sun had disappeared and had been replaced by a brown-grey sky. I drove and drove until we found ourselves in the Botanical Gardens.

Like a deflated rag doll, she climbed down from the van. Side by side, we walked. We passed scarlet arrowheads, maroon butterflies and stagnant ponds. On a stage, there was a school band playing honest-to-God folk. We bought a coffee, found a seat and settled close to the stage. Slyly, I watched her. Nerys's phone bleeped – crazy-bleeped. She switched it off.

My wife looked prettier than she had done last night when we'd piled back to Marchant's place. We'd fallen through the door like we owned the place – like we owned *his* place, could you credit it? But we couldn't have cared less where we were, and Marchant, well… he had a friendly way, and we needed a friend last night.

Nerys patted her support into my knee, and I waited for that old, familiar feeling to resurface. My gut gurgled. I listened to its thunder.

'So the cat fight yesterday?'

'Ah, she's a fiery one,' Nerys whispered. 'But her bark's worse than her bite. We're always having a set-to. It's our thing.'

But it had been my wife's flaming eyes that had scared me. And those wrists of her had been quick and strong. Sabina had been the fly caught in her web.

'You should see her when she's been at the vodka. Honestly, Duff, leave it? I don't feel – I'm squirming here. I need a bit of time. I just don't know what it is I want.'

Our conversation, the one that I had desperately wanted to have, was already half over, and soon it would be over for good. I wondered what then? I had liked Sabina, despite the threat she had posed to my plans, my wallet and my sanity.

Nonetheless, I wasn't ready to surrender my Nerys over to her.

Nerys rested her hand on my thigh. Nervously, I sipped my latte. My coffee tasted of earthy mud. What I wanted was some calming, soporific milk. Why couldn't they get it right, these barista people?

She needed time to think, she said. BRB, she said and I watched her move away from me. As for me, I pondered this delicate situation. It called for careful consideration. So, I pulled out my notebook. Weirdly, Nerys had never indicated to me, verbally or otherwise, that she found sex between us lacking. Nerys knew me better than anyone, better even than Cara – *of course better than Cara. Cara was NOT my sex partner. Are you shocked? I mean this merely as an observation, a statement of fact.* Cara was my daughter, but she'd never seen the whole of me. She'd only seen the shabby veneer. Nerys, though, she had seen me under the microscope, revelled in my small victories, my failures – *who knows? She'd tasted my skin, seen me cry, vomit, come, vomit-come, faint, stab a dying piglet* (a mercy killing, an act of terrible brutality that almost killed us both. I'll hear that tiny squeal to my dying day). My wife knew every crevice of my body: the scar under my belly-button, my webbed toes (second and third toes on both feet), the *disgusting, yellow dots on my tongue* that were a permanent fixture. As for me: I knew my wife's birth mark on her lower back, *like a coffee-stained tear,* her disproportionately long calves, *her watermelon buttocks.*

I chewed my pen. A baby sobbed on the bench behind. I

sensed all that had passed. *The curve of time that bends away from us. Cruel time that laughs at us stuck here like this. Tell us, how can we chase you, time? Where? Where did you go?* I remembered the farm with Cara, with Nerys, with Cwm's foggy eyes and Pepper's puce ring. *There was joy and hoping there. Never want to lose that. Where? Time, where did you go?*

Nerys, Sabina and me carried on up the coast. Crazy, I know, but Sabina had told us she had to see St Andrews and she had the kind of scowl neither of us could argue with. Sabina tailed us in her battered Citroen. Every few minutes, I smiled at her in the wing mirror. It was a chummy kind of smile, but it died unheeded in the haze. The wind wafted in and I breathed clearly again. Draping my arm out of the window, I proffered my thumbs skyward by way of support to the poor woman.

Sabina was a frightening woman, but she had a fine figure. Her stomach was plank-flat, her shoulders were sturdy and wide, like finely crafted brick-bats. From the van floor, I yanked a lager from its polythene and pulled the ring. The cracking sound was pleasing to hear and I took a long swig. For a second or two, I fooled myself into thinking a drop of lager could make me whole again. I didn't know why I had such lofty and unreasonable expectations of alcohol. You pull the ring and then what? It will all become clear? It will all turn from here?

I wanted to feel my blood warm, to be cleared of all the uncertainty, the pain, the agony. *Your brain, Duff; it's soft. You think it works the same as everyone else's, but it's… it's as cold and grey as the fog out of the window. The world doesn't always want to accommodate you. It tries to, but you don't make it easy for the world. It's not always the others who are in the wrong; sometimes it's you.*

'Duff? You with me? I was just saying I still don't know what to do.'

'About Sabina?'

'Of course about Sabina.'

Nerys kept her eyes on the road. Slowly, she licked her lips.

'You could always fight it out,' I said bitterly. 'Fight to the death, swing it so the feistiest bitch wins. You could beat my love rival any day,' I said. 'Leave her bloody and begging for mercy.'

At this, Nerys smiled. I wondered if this could have been the news she'd been waiting for. For me to declare myself a love rival. Had I not previously made my position clear? *This odd almost-marriage of ours: what is it? And just say a small child was travelling with us; what would a child make of us? Would they ask questions? Would they know we were two halves of the same whole? Together, and forever. And what of Cara? Was she so nonchalant last week because deep down she knew we belonged together?*

Nerys patted my knee and squeezed. She looked different now, but I wasn't sure how. Perhaps it was her purple heather lipstick. My wife smelt of peonies, freshly picked. As for me, I smelt strange. I sniffed under my arms. Warm and acidic.

I'd had tactics with women once upon a time. Perhaps, I

considered, I could hone them again. I used to know what to say to women. *But the elevator, it's sinking, Duff. Down, down it goes. How many floors now until you crash and crack your spine? Before your beating heart breaks for good?*

I turned to my wife. Sabina was no match for my wife in the style stakes. Sabina, in her tie-die tees and off-black Crocs, was in a different league. Some things I will never understand. I removed my wife's hand from my knee.

'What magic does she have, then? Okay, apart from the obvious. Give me three things – no, don't think! Off the top of your head… so you prefer vaginas?'

Nerys clicked her tongue against the roof of her mouth and glanced at me.

'It's not so simple, Duff. I really wish it was.'

She shifted down a gear and the van struggled along the last stretch of the motorway.

'So you actually like kissing girls? Their small mouths. The curve of the breasts. What about feeling small and protected? Don't you enjoy feeling vulnerable?' Aware I was rambling now, I rubbed my cheeks. She sucked her lip – playfully? 'So, tell me, when was the last time you saw her?'

'Ah, she came over. We had a bottle of wine. We sat at the laptop, sourced cheap materials. Looked into office space to produce our designs and – '

'When was this?'

'Duff. Driving, hon.'

'When?'

'If you must know, just before I came here.'

'And did you not think to tell her?'

'Nope, but if I told her where I was going. Back to you. Well... she wouldn't like it.'

She slid down the nearest exit. I saw blue shopping bags, wet feet, yellow road markings. Endless. My map was hidden under my seat, but I was in no mood to scoop it up and help her.

'So she's the jealous type?'

'God, yeah. Honestly, hon, it wouldn't have been worth it. It all happened so fast. Cara's call. Your desperate voice down the line. How was I to know she'd think I'd run off?'

Nerys slowed the van. I could see a car park; it was empty. The sea shone in the distance.

'Tell me, how did you meet?'

'Huh?'

'Seems a bit of a leap – no? Perfectly straight one minute, a lesbian the next.'

'Honey, I'm not a – '

'Who spoke to who?'

I waited.

'I wouldn't call myself a lesbian. I've just met someone I click with. Look, she chatted me up, if you must know. Not that it's any – '

'Aha, so Sabina was the keen one.'

Now we were getting somewhere.

We parked up in tandem with Sabina, and she treated us to a wide, American grin. I liked St Andrews. It was a city so much a part of the water it was like its jewelled bricks had sprung from the slime. All around us was glorious stonework and emerald green grass. Heavenly.

The students had disappeared, but you could feel their presence. I could imagine they were around the corner hiding in red robes, ready to jump out at us. We found a café, a place teeming with tourists. From the table at the window, I watched them pass: fat, thin, pasty, cold. I stirred my coffee and thought how much I'd enjoy putting a boot in the face of the golfer in the baby-blue polo shirt. I willed him to wind his chest in. Christ, the money, the sense of entitlement, and what do you do? You play golf.

Sabina ordered a slab of shortbread, chocolate-coated, speared with a tartan flag. I tutted. With Nerys outside making a call, I leaned across the marble table.

'What do you think?' I asked.

'Sure, it's cute,' she said, brushing crumbs from her T-shirt.

'Not the flag, dummy.'

I watched her open her bag and pull out a small pouch of American Spirit. She slammed it down on the table. Tiny red veins dotted her nose and her chin. I suspected she'd been blowing her lungs away for some time.

'About Nerys and me,' I said. 'Really sorry. You must be disappointed. A shock... Nerys not fill you in?

Hearing this, her dark eyes remained wide and cow-like. Unflappable.

'I knew about you guys.'

'?'

'Still married and all. Never got round to doing the deed, did you?' I watched her smile drop. As quick as a crack of thunder, she rolled a cig. Impressive. 'Still, why put yourself through it? That's what I said to her. Fleecing him's not nice. Of course, I said, the farm will have to go. We'll need the cash for the business. We're going to need all we can get.' She waved her tartan flag and brushed it along the neck of my jumper. 'I'm divorced, Duffy. I tell you, man, it's horrible. All that you have to do. Signing the darn forms. For ever and ever. Not what you expect at all. Sure, you can't stand the sight of them anymore, but it hurts, you know? You think it will last forever. That's the dream. We all buy into it at some time or other. Makes you sentimental to think back. That day when you said *I do*. Makes you wanna weep for your innocent self. Oh sure. The pain of knowing who you were then. It hurts bad, you know? So, I says to her: no, honey, you listen to me. If he insists on the paperwork, fine. But it's cool with me, whatever.'

'But this – it's not the – '

She spread her palm across my mouth. Her fingers smelt smoky. Her nails were bitten down to the wick.

'No, no need to explain, Duffy, I'm on your side too. I've been there, remember? I know how sucky all this can be. The heartbreak, the sorrow.'

She patted my hand. Thoughts circled in my head of where to turn, what to say, but I had no answers. She stood up and walked out of the door.

Over on the horizon, the sea was an enemy that followed me wherever I looked. If it was closer, I'd give it a good, hard kick. Overhead, seagulls shrieked *I told you so, Duffy, didn't I?*

A pang of homesickness. The mammoth journey back.

Sometimes I sit and I wait for my world to begin. When will it begin? When will it end? What choice do any of us have?

So, I sit alone and I wait. I study the body language between the She-Devil and my wife.

Sabina's feet face away from my wife in the direction of the sea. Nerys's feet point towards Sabina. Nerys grips her shoulder. Clumsily, the puffy-chested golfer returns, not looking where he's going and slices through the middle of them. Nerys steps aside. She turns around and looks at me with hard, hazel eyes.

Bam! I'm not worth it, her look says. I'm not worth giving up Sabina and the United States of America for. *What if… when this is all over, you stare into the void, Nerys. You're left with neither of us. It could happen.* We had a child together, *imperfect, glorious. Maybe you'd like another. Maybe a boy. His hair auburn, like my own. His thighs, strong, like yours, his shoulders straight. Make him a man, do all you can for him. Together, we'll bring him up. A kid needs two parents, if that's what we can be. And Cara, she hurt so bad. But we won't make the same mistake with the boy. No, it'll all be different this time, you'll see. Give me a chance, Nerys, give the boy a chance, give him an education, a proper one, no compromises, together forever, the four of us. A boy to play with. Not mess up. We can learn from our mistakes. Cara taught us all we know. We have time, we can do this Nerys, we can at least try.*

I watch them walk towards me. Their strides are the same, their rhythm is the same. I look down to Sabina's yellowing, stubby fingers as she hands me her key. *No excuses now, Duffy, you're well enough now, huh? No sense in the three of us squashed together in the van. I have to get the Citroen back down somehow. Must be with the one I love.*

So, I leave the café and follow them across the tarmac and back to the van parked in the dim shade. Nerys's chin shakes, but Sabina is as calm and undisturbed as the buildings rising to the sky behind her. By the van, Nerys kisses me softly on the cheek. Her flowery scent makes me weak. I take a step back. *Watch your legs move in time. My van. My museum piece. You clamber in. You take the wheel. Slowly, Sabina lifts my jacket from her feet. She mouths to me through the window. Do I need it for the journey? Will I be okay in just a sweater?*

In auto-pilot, with my brain stop-starting, I open the door of the Citroen behind.

The wide-brimmed hat rests on the back seat. A map of the USA, the same one you had attached to the mirror in the van, dangles by my nose. I sniff the sun-scorched cardboard. The engine grunts. I pull away. Ahead of me at the junction, you slow, indicate left. I follow. You speed up. Don't want to lose you.

There you go back to life a job money a home the loser follows the leader what I do is I follow like a lamb to the slaughter like a limpet to the rocks like a lemming to the cliff as a kid time stretches before you so much time goes on and on and you're born and you grow up and you look back and you have a past but being old is a long way off even though you're not the one swinging a dummy wetting your pants eating dirt pies sucking on teats you've left that far behind I used to think the future meant having all your problems solved as a kid you're a prisoner in at certain time in at five for your tea bath at seven bed by eight time bolts you down you want escape from the rules of time but time doesn't stop pinning you down that's the joke and it is a joke the joke is on me endings are important you start a book you anticipate an end it's what you expect life is surrender I see that now.

Acknowledgements

I owe a debt to my early and expert readers: Jonathan Barnes, Patricia Borlenghi, Tom Bromley, Lou Chandler, Justin Lewis, Ger Nichol, Phil Norman, Katy O'Brien and Scott Pack.